Cypriana

Atilla Tiriyaki

Ovester Publishing

Copyright © 2017 Atilla Tiriyaki. All rights reserved.

This work is registered with the U.S. Copyright Office

Cover design by OctagonLab

First Edition, 2017

A catalogue record for this book is available from the British Library

ISBN Number: 978-1-9997976-0-7

An eBook version of this book is also available

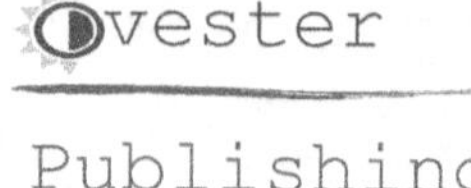

Published by Ovester Publishing, London

www.ovester.com/publishing

Special discounts are available for large quantity purchases. For further information, please email sales@ovester.com

For more information about the author, please go to www.atillatiriyaki.com

This book is dedicated to my mother, for without her, this book would have never happened. I would also like to thank my entire family for their unyielding love and support. Finally to my beautiful nieces, I hope that when you read this book, it provides you with some insight into the incredible culture you come from

Contents

Introduction

I would like to start off by thanking you for choosing my book.

Before we get into the story, I wanted to tell you a little about Cyprus and its people from my own personal experiences. Though some of the stories may not show people in their best light, however like in life, we sometimes do or say things that we might not necessarily mean. That said, I would highly recommend if you ever get the chance to go to Cyprus, to discover the people for yourself.

Yes, it is true that some of these people are slightly "crazy". However, they are also kind and funny, and it is fair to say that I have seen crazy people wherever I have travelled around the world, and I don't think Cyprus has the monopoly, just has more than the average quota.

The island, both North and South is stunning and over the past 10 years has seen a lot of changes, with the walls that once divided them, slowly coming down and hopefully one day the island will once again be unified. The 1974 war divided the island, ironically both the Greek and Turkish Cypriot cultures and people share so many similarities, and for the years prior to all of the troubles, the Greek and Turkish inhabitants of the island lived as neighbours and as friends. I have a lot of friends and family from both sides of the island, and for me, war is not about people, but countries and politics.

Now for the story…

Aziz is a 28-year-old American-born journalist living in London. He is originally from Los Angeles, however, moved to London after the devastating break-up of his relationship.

The story is set in 2003 and is based around the death of his grandfather, who died while visiting family in London.

Aziz faces a number of challenges from getting his grandfather's body back to Cyprus to Aziz being naturalised. However, the journey is centred around remembering his childhood in Cyprus, his family and the people he encounters along the way, who are not only slightly crazy but also very kind, hospitable and funny.

I hope that this book will make you laugh, but ultimately appreciate the cultural differences and similarities that all families go through when someone close to them dies.

Please enjoy!!!!

Atilla

Chapter One

You're In The Army Now

He's dead. Words that anyone with relatives abroad dreads, especially when it is over the phone and delivered from your charming cousin Mehmet. When you hear those words there is the fact that you will never see that person again, but there is also the nightmare of the funeral arrangements and having to face the hordes of relatives that you probably haven't seen in too many years to count.

"Oh no, when did Dede die."

"Don't know, last night", said Mehmet. He was never one for beating around the bush, what was surprising me more, was the fact that Mehmet was actually speaking. Typically he would just grunt or nod his replies to your questions, or if you were lucky, as in this case, he would use the fewest possible words to tell you what he needed to.

"How's Nene?" I asked. Our grandmother was four years younger than our grandfather but still in her late eighties and though relatively active, she was the sort of person that could make a motivational speaker take anti-depressants.

"Old, got to go bro", and with that Mehmet put down the phone.

What made my grandfather's death worse was the fact that he had died while visiting his daughter, my aunt Ayse, in London.

He always hated to leave his home in Cyprus and to die in London would have been his worst nightmare.

With grown up children and grandchildren all around the world, they would often reluctantly take short breaks to see the family, complaining the whole time that no one comes to visit them in Cyprus any more.

Given how much my grandfather had disliked travelling, I would have imagined that if my grandfather had felt his life slipping away, he would have held on and rushed back to Cyprus until his last dying breath, even passing away on the runway would have likely been much more preferable to him.

Once the plane had landed, I can imagine some poor unsuspecting stewardess approaching and asking why he hadn't left the plane, then screaming as she discovered his lifeless body, with a smile of contentment on his face.

Unfortunately for my grandfather, he had died in my cousin's bedroom in my aunt's house in North London, surrounded by countless posters of half-naked women on the walls, which were probably partly what killed him. Though he died peacefully in his sleep, he was still thousands of miles away from his beloved Cyprus.

★

Navigating deaths and marriages are complicated when you have a global family. If you are not careful, you can quickly start long feuds with family members, simply by not attending an event.

The next time they see you, it usually starts with, "you went to Gulsen's wedding, why didn't you go to Aydin's, don't you like her?"

My approach has always been simple, avoid every event and then the arguments won't happen. My mother, ever the opportunist, would typically make up some lie about how busy I am, and then begin boasting to anyone that would listen about her journalist son. However, this is the death of my grandfather and one I can't avoid.

My grandfather dying in London, caused further complications, as most of the family lived in Australia or America. Bar myself, a couple of younger cousins, which included the charming Mehmet and a really unhappy divorced aunt, whom I tried to avoid as much as possible, we were the only ones living in London.

Given that my grandfather had died in London and how few of us lived there, I immediately guessed I would be responsible for helping to sort out the travel and funeral arrangements.

Like with most Muslim funerals, burials take place in a relatively short time after death, so I knew that we had to get on with sorting things out. I immediately tried to call my grandmother, but the phone was constantly engaged, no doubt family members along with the fifth-cousin-twice-removed types desperately trying to find out how my grandmother was coping.

Failing to get through, I decided that rather than constantly redialling and trying to speak to my family before someone else did, I would be practical and call the travel agents to book the flights.

I went through the telephone directory and saw the details of a Turkish sounding travel agency and dialled the number. When I asked for the next available flight out to Cyprus, I was informed that they there were only three seats out for the following day, knowing someone within the family would use them, I decided to book all three.

Once all of the flight details had been confirmed, I sent a short text message to my aunt telling her not to worry about booking any flights. A short while after sending the text, my home phone began to ring.

"Aziz, it's your Nene", I had guessed that my aunt had received my text and informed my grandmother about the flights.

"Oh, Nene I am so sorry about Dede, are you okay?" for someone that is paid to express himself through words, I am not very good when people die and can never find the right words to say.

"He was old and trust him to die in London! He couldn't have waited until we got home, this is typical of him, he is so selfish, this is going to cost a lot to fly him back" she replied.

Considering my grandmother is in her eighties and was never formally taught English, she spoke surprisingly well. My grandfather, on the other hand, was much more fluent as he would typically always do most of the talking when they were together; "speaking to the white foreigners" as he would often say.

"Nene, it doesn't matter about the cost, we will all sort it out", with that all I could hear on the other end of a call was a kind of grunt of acknowledgement; although my grandmother loved her husband, she had almost seemed more upset about the inconvenience it had caused.

Of the two of them, my grandmother was always the one frugal with money, if it weren't for my grandfather, she would have likely been a millionairess. My grandfather was her opposite when it came to money, he was social and liked spending, whether it was through gambling or drinking.

Because of this, you would often hear the two of them arguing about my grandfather taking money from one of her many hiding places.

How he managed to find them, was always a mystery, either he would have made an amazing detective, or he just knew her too well. Most of the time, the shock of how he discovered her latest hiding place, suppressed the anger over the money being taken.

"The money was in the plastic bag, hidden inside the arse of chicken within the freezer, how did you know?" to which my grandfather would just grin and just give her a look akin to 'that is for me to know'.

My grandmother was little, about 4ft 2′ tall, slightly overweight and used a walking stick to get around. She would often use her age as both an excuse and a way of getting people to do what she wanted.

She recently avoided going to her niece's wedding because she hated her niece's future husband. She made no secret of it to everyone but her niece, often telling people "I don't like him, his eyes are too close together".

However, when she spoke to her niece she acted frail and confused "I wish I could come, however, I am getting so old, I am just so tired, and I don't know how long I have left".

With her children and grandchildren, guilt was something we were all used to as she would often say "When are you coming to Cyprus, I am not going to be around much longer you know". Though you would immediately feel guilty, she had done it so often over the years that everyone became slightly immune to it.

"What time is the flight Aziz?" my grandmother asked. I had actually managed to book the closest thing to a direct flight to Northern Cyprus.

"It's at 3 pm tomorrow Nene, from London Stansted Airport" with that she said "Ok" as she put down the phone.

As soon as I put the phone down, it began to ring again.

"Sorry Aziz, I told my mother I wanted to speak to you, but she hung up, she never listens! I just wanted to say thanks for booking the flights and to let you know I have arranged for your Dede's body to be flown back to Cyprus. It will hopefully be on the same flight as us tomorrow" said aunt Ayse.

"You okay?" I asked

"I will be better when I know Dad is back safely in Cyprus". Though she was clearly upset, she was in organiser mode, and after a short conversation, we both said goodbye.

That night I got very little sleep, I had tried until very late to get hold of my parents who lived in Los Angeles with no luck, and even though I wanted to call around, I decided not to, as it was likely most of the family would be frantically booking flights over to Cyprus.

When I woke the following morning, and after my fourth coffee, I realised how quickly the time was going and decided that I should arrange a taxi to take me to the airport.

By the time the taxi arrived, I was so tired, that if I sat down for too long, I would likely pass out, so I made small talk with the taxi driver to keep me awake as he drove me to Stansted airport.

The taxi driver was extremely chatty, he did go quiet for a little while when he had assumed that I was going on holiday after I told him where I was travelling to. When I clarified it was for a funeral, you could see him trying to find a way back from his mistake.

When I arrived at the airport it was a bit of a mad rush, having not allowed too much time to get to the airport, it was all a bit tight. I had called my aunt from the taxi, in which she eventually answered after 4 attempts.

My aunt had a mobile phone, which was expensive to use. After her son Mehmet racked up a £300 bill on it in one month, she would now only use it for absolute emergencies. She would also often forget that she had it, as no one ever called her on it.

When I finally got through, I told my aunt and grandmother to check-in to the flight as I wasn't going to be sitting with them as I was going to get a smoking seat.

After running to the check-in desks and having the agent telling me off that I should try to arrive at least 2 hours before departure, I was finally given a boarding pass. I quickly went through security and made my way to the gate, which had already come up on the departures board as boarding.

★

Once I had arrived at the gate I knew it was my flight, you could tell by the scowling looks of the people waiting at the gate. A lot of Turkish people have a habit of staring at you, staring so intensely that you know that it is not a passing glance and by looking at their faces you know exactly what they are thinking. It is usually a look of disgust or disappointment, a look you too often see from your own family.

As I made myself comfortable, a sort of golf cart pulled up to the gate, as it came to a stop, I saw my grandmother and aunt slowly getting out. My grandmother looked so frail and walked at such a snail's pace that it seemed that every step was pure agony for her.

I made my way over and gave the traditional Turkish greeting of kissing them on both cheeks, which is common in greeting men, women, friends and family.

Given my grandmother's condition, we were among the first to board. As we made our way up to the gate to board the plane, I glanced around and saw the looks of hatred of the other passengers at the fact we got to board before them, and once on the aircraft, I made my way back to my smoking seat.

After the masses had all squeezed their bags, boxes, clothing and anything else they could fit in the overhead compartments, the air stewardess began the ritual of telling you what to do in case of an emergency.

It was hard to see any expression on the stewardesses faces given the amount of makeup they were wearing. It was like when a young girl first starts experimenting with makeup and decides to put everything on to shock their parents.

The air stewardesses were known to have an attitude and on one flight out to Cyprus when I was 15, the stewardess told a passenger to sit down rudely, as she pushed him down into his seat. She was telling him to wait until the plane had properly stopped and to remain seated.

The passenger clearly did not like being told what to do or being manhandled in this way and decided to take a swing at her, he punched her so hard that the force knocked her to the ground and she was immediately unconscious. This was Cyprus in the 90s, the other passengers gave no reaction and stepped around her to exit the plane. After the event, I never found out what happened to the passenger or the air stewardess.

Shortly after the aircraft had taken off, I decided to light up a cigarette and as soon as I had taken the first drag the man from the seat in front turned around. He began to moan, stating how it was illegal to smoke on flights, at the same time trying to get the attention of one of the airline staff. He seemed to be like your stereotypical uptight British person abroad, probably on route to look at the various religious sites within Cyprus.

"Actually, you can smoke on most routes to and from Turkey" I replied, even though I was explaining to him that the airlines in Turkey had not yet implemented a no smoking ban on their flights, it was evident he was not listening to me. It was only when the air stewardess turned up and told him that "Is smoking seat" and swiftly walked off, that he had realised what I had said was true.

The flight time was six hours, three and a half hours to Istanbul, one-hour refuelling and one and a half hours to Cyprus. The route was classified as direct, as ever since the 1974 war, all airlines to Northern Cyprus had to stop off in Turkey before they were able to fly on to the only airport in Northern Cyprus, Ercan Airport.

The lack of sleep had caught up with me, and as I was the only person seated in a row with three seats, I decided to stretch out and close my eyes for a little while.

I was woken up by two young men trying to sit down where my legs were spread out. In my daze, I quickly realised we had arrived in Istanbul, so what I thought was a quick snooze, had actually been three hours. I wasn't surprised as it is common for travellers to leave and join the flight in Istanbul as the plane continued onto Cyprus.

Though I was still hal asslep, I sat up and moved over to my seat, as soon as the guys sat down, a strong smell of body odour and cigarettes came wafting over; it was unbearable.

They were both young, but they look liked they had just stepped out of the seventies, with longish hair and flares. My guess is that they were being made to do national service in Cyprus and the next day they would probably be in army issued uniforms with skinheads, so they were likely making the most of the freedom while they could.

I tried to position my nose in various directions to see if I could avoid the smell, however no matter what direction I tried, the smell was still there, ever strong. I reassured myself that I only had an hour and a half to go, but it wasn't helping.

As I slept for most of the journey, the air stewardess came over and thrust a tray with undisclosed food on it. I tried to establish what it was but decided that with only a short while to go I would wait until I arrived in Cyprus to eat. I offered my meal to the two men, though they were surprised by my offer they were happy to help me by clearing the tray

At last, we had landed, the passengers erupted in cheers and began clapping, and it was as though they were not expecting to arrive as safely or as smoothly as they had.

Before the plane had come to a stop, everyone began jumping up from their seats, it was survival-of-the-fittest with everyone pushing and shoving.

The British man in the seat in front looked on in shock and horror like he was expecting everything to be done in an orderly fashion.

I pushed my way up to the front of the plane to be close to where my grandmother and aunt were seated. Once the doors opened, everyone made a dash for the door, though everyone was eager to get out, the hordes of people still held back, allowing all of the old and frail to exit first.

My grandmother was one of the first to leave, making her way down the stairs, taking one step at a time. She was already wearing a black headscarf, which is common when a woman is a widow and was looking even frailer than she had in London.

The plane had taxied close to the terminal, and as it was within walking distance, people were making their own way to the terminal building. Given my grandmother's condition, I began speaking to the ground crew about arranging some transportation.

13

As soon as I starting speaking, I heard my grandmother shouting with excitement and as I turned around, this little old, frail lady having seen someone she recognised had suddenly become a 100-meter sprinter, her legs and walking stick in unison as she sprinted to the terminal building.

"Nene, where are you going?" I cried out, but it seemed like she did not hear as she did not look back.

After looking like a liar, I apologised to the ground crew and decided to catch up with her and enter the terminal building.

★

Northern Cyprus is an army state, so on arrival, you are greeted by soldiers rather than immigration officials when it comes to checking your passport.

When it was our turn, the three of us went up to the counter and handed our passports to the soldier. Before he even had a chance to look at the first passport, my grandmother began telling her life story. The soldier was clearly not listening and spent most of his time looking down.

"Is this your grandson?" the soldier asked looking directly at my grandmother

"Yes, this is Aziz, he is a journalist in London", my grandmother had replied with such pride, "Was his mother or father born in Cyprus?"

"Yes, why?" my grandmother replied.

"He will need to become a citizen and register with the Army" and with that he handed us back out passports as we made our way to the arrivals hall.

Chapter Two

Where's The Body?

Adem, a second-cousin, had volunteered to come and collect us from the airport. It wasn't hard to spot Adem in the arrivals hall, as he was standing there talking to a small group of people, all of whom seemed to be hanging onto to his every word. This was a familiar scene with Adem, as he was a well-liked, very charismatic and funny man, with a lot of friends across the island.

Adem was one of my grandfather's favourite nephews, and he would often talk about him with high regard. These feelings were also reciprocated, as Adem would do anything for his beloved uncle, often utilising his vast network of friends to get the best deals for his uncle.

The moment Adem had spotted us, he came running over, immediately greeting my grandmother and then my aunt. When it was my turn, he decided to carry out some sort of wrestling move, which clearly did not go as he had intended and it just resulted in him messing up my hair.

As we made our way to the airport's car park, it wasn't hard to spot Adem's car. For as long as I can remember, he had driven a large golden coloured Mercedes Benz. The car was actually older than me and though Adem had customised it with a horn that played about 100 different sounds, what he had failed to do was to fix the suspension.

Taking a ride in his car was never a comfortable experience, and as soon as you were seated, you would immediately feel each and every one of the springs from within the car seat. Any time he drove over a bump or through a ditch in the road, it would immediately result in the seat springs being thrust even deeper into the unsuspecting passenger's arse cheeks.

When he drove through a large bump in the road, I looked over to my aunt Ayse, and it was clear that she was having a similar experience to me from the look of grimace on her face, but my grandmother and Adem seemed somehow immune to the springs' effects.

Looking around the car, it was hard not to be drawn to the furry dashboard and dice hanging from the mirror. I kept on trying to work out what use a furry dashboard has; it can't be for show, as it looks strange… maybe somewhere to wipe your hands when they sweat or insulation during cold winter nights' maybe?

"What is the weather like Adem?" my grandmother asked, clearly making small talk.

"About 32 degrees aunty", Adem replied.

Adem drove an automatic car due to an incident that had occurred in his youth. In his twenties, he was having an affair with a married woman, and it all came to a sad end when the husband of the woman he was having an affair with, caught them in the act.

The story of how it happened was common knowledge, as Adem would freely tell anyone that would ask. He would explain that the women's husband, on discovering his wife in a compromised position, was not amused and went to his car to fetch his gun.

Adem and the husband fought for some time, and when telling the story, it was at this point that Adem would begin to laugh. He would go on to say that during the fight, the wife, who was still naked, was screaming from the bed, supposedly telling her husband not to get shot, showing little regard for the man she had just slept with.

During the struggle, the gun went off. It was only when both men had moved away from each other that it became apparent that the weapon had been pointing at Adem's arm when it went off.

Adem screamed at the woman to throw over his pants as in all of the commotion, he hadn't realised that he had been fighting with the man naked and didn't like the idea of being taken to hospital in just his birthday suit.

Realising Adem was the one that had been injured, anger soon turned to panic as the husband began worrying about himself and whether he would end up in prison. What made it worse was that the husband was actually a police officer, and he had used his police issued firearm.

Once Adem was taken to the hospital, it was quickly determined that the damage had been so great that the doctor had no choice but to amputate the arm.

Even with one arm, Adem was still very upbeat and blamed no one, he would freely admit that he brought his misfortune upon himself. The husband ended up just getting a severe telling off as Adem insisted that he did not want to press charges and with that, the case was dropped.

Ironically once all of the drama had calmed down, the police officer and his wife decided to make a go of it and over time became close friends with Adem. That said, I don't think the husband ever left the two of them alone again in the same room.

I couldn't stop thinking about what happened at the airport. I had a sick feeling in my stomach as we drove through village after village. All of these questions were swirling around my head, I wasn't sure what it meant to be naturalised, how it would affect me when I travelled, what I would have to do. I was also an American citizen, and dual nationality was and has always been complicated.

All I knew of being naturalised was the fact that I would likely have to do National Service. National Service in Cyprus was a gruelling 2 years or if you were over a certain age, a mere one month. Neither option appealed to me.

I started imagining all of these images, of being like the guys on the plane, making my way to the army base, being issued with my uniform and having my hair shaved. Being shouted at and taunted for being American by my drill sergeant, probably some loud, overweight, moustachioed with bad meat breath sergeant. What was I going to do?

"Don't worry Aziz, I am sure one of your uncles will go with you to sort out your naturalisation" said aunt Ayse, who could clearly see I was worried and thought that offering the company of one of my crazy uncles might help to ease my mind.

"Thanks but I am not worried, I was just thinking". I was lying but didn't want to start getting people worried about me, when they had bigger things to worry about.

★

Kyrenia is one of a few cities in Northern Cyprus and is located on the northern coastline of Cyprus. Famous for its historic harbour, castle and in more recent times, for its restaurant, bars and hotels.

My grandparents, though both originally from small villages in Famagusta, had bought land in Kyrenia just after the war. Kyrenia was always a popular tourist resort before and after the war, but it was about one hour's drive from the airport, which is considered a long journey, given the size of the island. For that reason, they also kept their village house in my grandfather's childhood village, and they would split their time between the two houses.

Given the route we were taking, it had seemed that Adem believed we had wanted the scenic tour, as he had decided to take us the long way round, going through countless villages as he drove through the mountain on his way to Kyrenia. If he had taken the new highway, our journey would have taken a lot less time.

The government was still in the process of constructing the new highway, so parts were still like dirt roads, but there were also parts that now had freshly laid tarmac, which if Adem had taken that route, it would have at least given my arse a few moments of light relief from the springs.

It was typical for projects in Cyprus to take a lot longer than they should. Though there was a completion date for the highway, everyone would just laugh it off as they knew it would take three times longer than stated, given the number of officials involved and the fact that the money for the construction was being funded from Turkey.

Except for the three cities of Nicosia, Famagusta and Kyrenia, most of Northern Cyprus is made up of clusters of villages. These villages are generally close from one another, but each has its own identity and community pride, especially when it comes to football. For nearly all of the villages across Cyprus have its own football team, which will be made up of young men from the local community. Football matches, official and unofficial were frequent, and rivalries between villages were also very common.

Not only that but in most villages, you would also find that the vast majority of the inhabitants of that village are from three or four prominent families, so typically, everyone in the community is related.

It also gets a little confusing, as most villages have three names, a Greek name from before, a current Turkish name and a nickname. Northern Cypriots love to give nicknames to people and places, so locals don't always call individuals, things and places by their given names.

You will often hear nicknames of villages based on the perceived characteristics, like one village is known for being tight with money and another known for lying. The nicknames are known by everyone and are typically used when someone is explaining a person's behaviour, like "see he is from the village of liars" or "what do you expect from a village where they are tight with money".

My grandfather's village was one that had previously had more Greeks inhabitants than Turkish and bordered both the Nicosia and Famagusta regions. My grandparents spoke both Greek and Turkish, and whenever they wanted to talk to each other without anyone understanding, they would talk to each other in Greek, as their children only knew a handful of words.

★

Like a lot of people, my grandfather found the war hard, not only was there death and decay all around but friends turned on friends. Even up until the day he died, he struggled to sleep given the horrific things he had seen. He would often explain that seeing the effects of war was bad enough, but even worse when you knew the people, especially those you considered friends.

In the '90s, a lot of younger Turkish Cypriots that were not even born during the war had started to have anti-Greek Cypriot attitudes. If my grandfather ever heard any remarks or comments, he would get really annoyed.

He would tell them all the same story, about a Greek man in his village that was part of the Greek Cypriot army. On discovering that there were a number of Greek troops heading towards my grandfather's village, he put his own safety on the line and told my grandfather to get out, saving not only my grandfather but also his family.

This was not uncommon, and there were similar stories from Greek Cypriot friends, where Turkish Cypriot soldiers did the same thing for their friends and families.

As a journalist you are trained to keep impartiality, and over the years I would often hear both sides of the argument, and in the end, I came to the same conclusion, war is war.

As we passed through the villages, I remember one of the things that I love about Cyprus. Though there are lights in various villages, typically they are not street lights, but lights from people's homes. For extended periods of time, there would be total darkness, except for the passing vehicle headlights. During these periods of total darkness, it made it so easy to see the stars in the sky, so clear and shining brightly. Living in London and growing up in Los Angeles, though the stars could be seen at night, they were never as clear as they were in Cyprus.

The darkness was coupled with the sounds of insects and the fresh air; rich with the smell of olives, and often farmyard smells, as you drove past the villages.

"We are here". At last the car pulled up to my grandparents' home. As we walked up to the veranda, I could begin to feel the pressure of my arse ease, as it was now no longer subjected to the torture of the seat springs.

Once we were on the veranda, all my childhood memories came flooding back, countless holidays with my cousins', over visiting my grandparents and all the mischief we would get up to. I began to laugh as I remembered my grandfather sitting on the veranda listening to the radio and smoking. People would see him from the street as they passed by, stop at the gate to the house to talk to him. It would typically start off civil but would inevitably end up with my grandfather shouting at them to go away, usually not so politely, after they had disagreed with him about something.

The house was a single storey four-bedroom property dwarfed by the surrounding mansions. The house was in the hills of Kyrenia and thought of as an affluent area. People would often tell my grandfather to build a bigger property on his land, but my grandfather was always the kind of man to be defiant of perceptions. He would say "why should I build a seven bedroom house, just because the idiots around me have."

As we entered the house, my grandmother went straight into the kitchen and sat down on the minder. A minder, which is pronounced min-deh, is a sort of bench with cushions on, and typically every Turkish home has one. They are the place people would take naps on, where families would sit and in my grandmother's case, a place for storage. Under my grandmother's minder, you would often find melon, large containers of olive oil, flip flops and countless other small items.

"You should get some rest Aziz", my grandmother said as she directed me to the second of the four bedrooms.

"I will Nene, you should rest too".

After brushing my teeth and washing up, I went into the room. The bedroom summed up my grandparent's taste, white walls, flowery curtains and white cotton bedding with lace, simple with some traditional elements.

It was so hot in the room that I immediately turned on the ceiling fan. I was so exhausted that I collapsed on the bed and fell to sleep straight away.

I woke up the next day to the smell of fried food. I felt so rested, a feeling I hadn't felt for a very long time. The house was so peaceful that even outside there was not a single sound. After getting dressed, I made my way to the kitchen.

"Good morning Nene", just by looking at what she had been doing, it was evident that she had been up for some time. My grandmother had always said that she wakes up automatically with each sunrise, something that she has done ever since she was a little girl. Her early morning routine was typical for a lot of older Cypriots, as growing up in Cyprus, all of the family members were required to tend to their animals, which meant early morning starts.

My grandmother was already busy setting the table, preparing a typical Cypriot breakfast of fresh bread, fried Turkish cheese known as helim (also known as halloumi), fresh cucumber, olives and watermelon.

My grandmother made her own helim throughout the year and would put both the old and newly made helim in brine to preserve it. Unfortunately, preservation made it hard, so though it was ideal for frying or cooking with, to eat it uncooked made it tough, and people were known to lose a tooth or two if they tried.

"Eat, eat" she said as I came close to the table, pulling out a chair, ushering me to sit down. The chair was the one that my grandfather would typically sit at. I moved to a different seat as didn't feel right to sit there. My grandfather always sat at the head of the table, not that we would see him sitting there often. Every time I visited over the years, you would rarely see him, as he would often be drinking and socialising at the local café. This time though, I knew that he wasn't at the café, and it started to make his death a lot more real.

As I started to load my plate with cheese and bread, my aunt Ayse walked in.

"Bloody mosquitos, it is way too hot, and someone was snoring so loudly last night". It was clear to see that my aunt had been the main course for the mosquitos, just by looking at the four visible bites on her arm, which she was frantically scratching as she sat down.

Though aunt Ayse had remarked about the snoring, we all knew that it was my grandmother who had been snoring like a boar. It was a family joke that my grandmother was known to snore when she slept, but she was also known for blaming my grandfather for the sounds, even if there were no way it could have been him.

"Aziz will you come with me later to get dad's body?. He should have arrived by now, and I need to find out what we need to do next". My aunt's request was more out of not wanting to face it alone, and I couldn't blame her.

"Of course Aunt, do you want me to drive?" Driving in Cyprus was a prospect I did not relish. On the roads, the drivers typically make their own rules, and you need your wits about you.

"If you don't mind" she replied as she put in a difficult to chew, piece of helim into her mouth.

★

My grandfather had two vehicles, a late 1960s Volkswagen Karmann coupé, which he used as his get around town car and a 10-year-old Volvo that was more for special occasions. Given the journey and wanting some comfort, I decided to take the Volvo.

On the drive up to Nicosia, my aunt would not stop talking, telling me about her work, her sons, and her ex-husband, and although I was nodding at the appropriate times, I actually didn't register much of what she was saying. I was trying not to be rude, as my aunt wasn't a bad person, but she did have the tendency to be very focused on herself. She was the type of person that if you told her that you failed an exam, her response would be "What am I going to tell people?!"

"Aziz, it is good what you are doing". My aunt's comment completely surprised me as I hadn't expected it

"It really is nothing aunty" I replied, but I was just glad that I was listening at that point to have been able to respond correctly.

As we got closer to Nicosia, I could hear the priest's mid-morning call to prayer. It was a sound you would often hear in every village all over Northern Cyprus. It brought back a memory of when I was really young and at a time when I didn't fully understand that it was a call to pray and not a song.

On one occasion when I was 6 years old, I began singing along and dancing to the morning prayer. Immediately I saw my grandfather's disgust, "Sit down you stupid boy, it is a prayer, didn't your mother teach you anything?" he rebuked.

★

Once we arrived in Nicosia, we made our way to an official looking government building, it was large and looked like it was in need of some repairs.

Once inside the main hall, the receptionist told us to go over to one of the clerks who would be able to help. As we got closer, we could see a balding clerk slumping behind his large wooden desk. The desk was a mess, there was paperwork, old newspapers and dirty cups covering every inch of the surface of the desk.

"Have a seat, what do you want?" the clerk said abruptly as we sat down.

After giving the clerk all of my grandfather's details, he got off and left his desk, taking the paperwork with him. After what felt like a long time, he eventually returned holding a folder and sat back down behind his desk.

"He is not in Cyprus", he said in a rather unsympathetic manner

"Where in the hell is he then?" I responded. I could see my aunt beginning to shake as she was trying to control and suppress her surprise and anger.

"Don't know, try speaking to the airline."

Like many of the government officials I had encountered over the years, this clerk had an air of arrogance about him, as if any action was an inconvenience or that he was doing some sort of favour for us.

My aunt leant across the desk so that her face was close to the clerk's and said: "Where the hell is my father's body?"

Chapter Three

What Do You Want?

In all of the commotion, I realised that I hadn't really thought about the fact that my grandfather had died. Suddenly a wave of emotions came over me, when I thought about the fact that I would never be able to see or speak to him ever again. Mixed in was also an element of guilt, as the last time I saw my grandfather, our encounter didn't go so well.

On my grandfather's previous trip to London, I went round, as I typically would do, to visit them, and no sooner had my grandfather finished with the formality of greeting me, he began complaining about the fact that none of the children or grandchildren ever came out to visit them in Cyprus.

While my grandfather was moaning, I made the mistake of briefly looking over to Mehmet, who was sitting there with his arms crossed, obviously bored. Once Mehmet had realised that I was watching, he looked straight at me and mouthed "Cos it is shit".

I couldn't help it and immediately began roaring with laughter. Although Mehmet may have been brave enough to have made such remarks behind my grandfather's back, he would have never had the courage to have said it loud enough for him to hear.

My laughter seemed to agitate my grandfather, and he quickly started to complain about how my father had allowed me to become more American, and as a result, that I had forgotten my heritage.

Though my grandfather typically got on well with my father, whenever it was something he didn't like or agree with, it was always my father's fault. He would go into a rant about some issue, how it was always my father's doing or lack thereof and how my mother was blameless and as much a victim, as everyone else.

Generally, he would stop after a short while and move onto the next subject, but on this occasion, he didn't stop and just kept on going.

"Just because your father's family are not good to one another, he wants his children to grow up the same way" he said.

I was not trying to be disrespectful, but I couldn't take it anymore. I jokingly said to my grandfather that my mother loved America as much as my father and with that, my grandfather erupted.

"Your father has turned your mother against her family and her country", by this point he was shouting rather than speaking.

"Dede, both my parents love their families, and growing up, they both always talked about their love for Cyprus" I replied.

"That is a lie! Your father couldn't wait to take your mother away from us" my grandfather bellowed. He was by now getting red in the face, which began to worry me, as given his age, I didn't want to be the cause of him having a heart attack.

Seeing the situation escalate, my grandmother came rushing into the room to diffuse the situation. Ever the diplomat she said: "Stop, it doesn't matter, it is their lives to do as they wish."

Realising my grandmother was probably intervening for a good reason and given that he realised that he was on the verge of likely saying something he might later regret, he seemed to start to calm himself down and began changing the subject.

He started to talk about immigration situation in the UK, which quickly got his temper up again.

"These illegal immigrates should be…" I knew what he was going to say, but by this point, I had begun switching off and started nodding. I was just thankful that he had changed the subject.

My grandfather's temper was known by everyone. It is typical, that as people get older, they tend to become more outspoken. However for my grandfather, he had actually started off being outspoken, so with him, the older he got, the more extreme both his moods and arguments became.

The only thing that was strange, was that although he was getting more and more outspoken, he seemed to be generally mellowing towards his immediate family.

It was probably a culmination of being aware that he was getting older and with each year and each new pain, the realisation that one day, perhaps even soon, he would have to start relying on his family to look after him.

That and the older he got, the more he thought about his own mortality and what follows, probably made him want to rack up a few brownie points being a kind and supportive parent and grandparent, something that he clearly was less worried about when he was younger.

Though most of the time he would erupt over really small things, the older he got, the quicker he seemed to calm down and change the subject. This approach was sometimes so sudden that you would be sitting there questioning whether what you had just witnessed, had actually happened. The man that only two seconds before was screaming about something was now sitting there laughing about the weather.

This new-found level of restraint was something that everyone in the family noticed, and a number of the younger family members would love to test the boundaries. They would typically start talking about Cyprus and something that could potentially tarnish the image my grandparents had of it.

My cousin Dilan once told my grandfather that he heard through friends that girls in Cyprus, in a desire to preserve their virginity would prefer to have anal sex.

As soon as Dilan had finished the sentence, my grandfather went from calm to being enraged in seconds.

"You stupid boy, that is not true, Turkish girls are not like that, they wait until marriage before having sex, you stupid..." before he could finish the sentence, my grandmother gave him a look, and he stopped himself from completing it.

Though the cousins loved to antagonise their grandfather, when he was in a mood, or they pushed it too far, they would all retreat, leaving my elderly grandmother to calm the situation.

Like many of my cousins, my relationship with my grandparents was slightly strange. We would typically see them over the 3-month summer holidays. Once we were in Cyprus, we would only really see them in the evenings, as for most of the day we would be outside playing with friends and family around the village or on the many acres of land my grandparents owned.

Most of us were closer to our grandmother, and I don't think any of the grandchildren had a particularly great relationship with our grandfather. That wasn't for want of trying from his perspective; he would often play the joker for our amusement, usually at our grandmother's expense, poking and prodding her, to get a reaction. However, he naturally was a serious man, very loudly spoken, often to the point of shouting and usually in some sort of disagreement with someone, well anyone really.

The older I got, the more I realised that much of my grandfather's behaviours were more because he grew up in a different era and some of his mannerisms were born out of his early life experiences. From the stories my mother told us as children, he didn't get on that well with his father and was often punished and made an example for his younger siblings to see. It seemed his mother had some sort of post-natal depression with my grandfather that she had carried with her from the day he was born. My mother would describe her grandmother as seeming to hate her father.

My mother would often tell us that her father was a lot worse when she was a child and that he actually was a lot more tender and loving towards his grandchildren. Given what I had seen of him, I didn't want to imagine what he was like with his own children.

As a toddler, the family would laugh whenever my grandfather was around, as I would generally hide behind my mother or cry when my grandfather tried to interact with me. I don't think anyone could blame me; this tall, white-haired, loud person, would likely scare anyone, let alone a young child.

Having said all that, we all knew our grandfather was a good man, it was just when he got in a mood, we would all run and hide for cover.

★

My family and their ways always seemed very alien to my non-Turkish friends. This became apparent when once of my closest friends in the neighbourhood once came over when my grandfather was visiting. We walked in at the point in which my grandfather was explaining to my mother what the flight over to the US was like. However, we swiftly left, as when I looked over, my friend looked scared.

When we went outside, he immediately asked me if everything was okay and why my grandfather was arguing with my mother. I told him that he wasn't arguing, but just talking.

For an outsider looking in, our expressive nature, strange sounding language and tactile approach to each other, must seem so different. I often imagined my friends going home and telling their families about the weird and crazy things that they had seen while visiting my home.

"They all kiss each other on the cheek, men and women, they eat plants..." and their families all listening to the strange tales about their Turkish neighbours.

Even for someone that is Turkish, the first time I ever went to Istanbul on holiday and saw two men holding hands, both my cousin and I laughed. My mother quickly informed us that in Turkish culture, good male friends hold hands, it isn't sexual, just an expression of solidarity and kinship. However, to two 8-year-old boys, it was funny and strange.

For me, growing up in both worlds, I understood American culture, as well as all the Turkish traditions, so would think nothing of the contrast. At times, I would get taken aback when someone asked a question about something they had seen or heard at my home, especially if they happened to walk in when the family were watching television.

As a family, we knew that if you wanted to watch television, you didn't do it when my grandparents were around. If it were the news, my grandfather would shout at the TV, like he was speaking directly to the reporter. I remember a news story in the US about a man that had tried to steal from a grocery store and the clerk from the store, had managed to grab the thief and wrestled him to the ground.

My grandfather roared with laughter and said "Bloody idiot, what sort of man is he? Is he stupid? What did he try to steal?"

He was asking so many questions as if the reporter would suddenly reply in the news item "He is unemployed, he is stupid, and he was trying to steal a pack of beers!"

It was bad enough watching the news with my grandparents, but Turkish soap operas were a big no-no. You would typically have my grandmother asking lots of questions

"Why is he standing on the cliff? Who is that girl?" and my grandfather talking the whole way through about the characters and how ridiculous it all was.

The constant talking throughout TV shows isn't uncommon for Turkish families, and this is typically why you have more than one TV in every home. One for the older Turks to scream at and one for the younger ones, so that they can watch their programmes in peace.

Looking at my grandparents, I always believed that it was an older generation thing, as my parents had never exhibited those sort of behaviours, however, the older my mother got, the more she started to show signs of 'TV interaction disorder', at least that is what I called it.

The 'disorder' first appeared while watching a sci-fi film at home when I was in my late teens. Fifteen minutes into the movie, my mother started to ask who the characters were and what was it all about. As the years went on, it got worse, my mother would swear that she had seen a movie, only to find out she hadn't, or half way through would suddenly say that she had watched it before.

My mother would hate to acknowledge it, but her personality was similar to that of her fathers', particularly his strong will and, on occasion, his temper. Unlike my grandfather though, my mother was a lot softer and loving. We all knew though that she had a side to her, that when she was in a temper, we would all run for cover. In that sense, my father was more like my grandmother and would calm my mother down.

We all knew that my parents had met at college, so on one particular day, I remember asking my grandmother about how she and my grandfather had met. When my grandmother starting telling me the story, she said that on the first time of ever seeing my grandfather, she had actually told her friend that she thought he was a bit of a fool and was not someone that she could have considered having a relationship with.

My grandparents had lived in neighbouring villages, which were about a thirty-minute walk or ten minutes by car. There was a four years age gap between grandparents, which meant that they had not been in the same year at school nor had the same circle of friends.

On one trip to my grandmother's village to watch a football match, my grandfather walked past my grandmother's house and saw her hanging washing in the garden. He later said that the moment he saw her, he was obsessed with her and immediately began thinking of ways to be introduced to her.

The following day, he started asking all of his friends in the village who this beautiful woman was. My grandfather's enquiries didn't go unnoticed, and it quickly came to the attention of my great grandfather.

The first time my grandparents actually met, my grandmother was outside with her mother, aunts, neighbours and cousins drinking coffee, when my grandfather purposely walked past the house, in an attempt to get a glimpse of my grandmother.

He walked past not realising that they were sitting outside the house, however upon seeing them he had no choice but to greet them all. He had been unaware that my great grandfather was home and had heard this young upstart speaking to his daughter. My great-grandfather came out and shouted for my grandfather to come inside and drink coffee with him.

Years later, my grandmother found out that her father interrogated her potential suitor, particularly regarding his intentions. My grandfather said the interrogation was so bad, that he was trying to hide the fact he was shaking. Shortly after the encounter, my grandfathers' family came around to express interest in my grandmother.

Once the interest had been shown, the two families got to know each other better, and it gave my grandmother and grandfather a chance to meet properly and get to know each other better. Any meetings between them were always chaperoned, and unfortunately for my grandfather, the chaperone was my grandmother's first cousin Meryem. Meryem was eagle-eyed, and no matter what they were doing, her eyes were firmly on my grandfather.

On one date, my grandfather took my grandmother to see a film. Half way through the movie, he looked over to see if Meryem was watching him and most likely to see if had an opportunity to make a sneaky move on my grandmother. As soon as he looked over, he realised that Meryem wasn't actually watching the film. Instead, she had her sights firmly fixed on him, so any hope of making a move quickly diminished.

Even after my grandparents married, my grandfather still disliked Meryem or the "nosy old bag" as he referred to her as. The feeling was mutual, and whenever she would come around and visit my grandmother, Meryem and my grandfather would bicker with one another.

Though my grandmother had initially thought my grandfather was a bit of a fool, she weighed up the fact that he came from a good family and given that he was well educated and had a good government job, she knew that he would be a great provider.

Even back then, my grandmother was pragmatic and decided that with all the factors in place, the least she could do is to see where this relationship could take them. My grandmother once told me that it took her at least one year into her marriage, to realise that she loved him.

Thinking back over my life, I realised that I never really had a long conversation with my grandfather. My encounters were either him ranting or joking about. Most of what I knew of him was third hand, from what his friends told me when I visited the village cafe, conversations with my mother or grandmother about what he was like, but nothing directly from him.

He was a private man in many areas, but one thing he did like to do, was to boast. He was often caught exaggerating about the successes of his grandchildren. My cousin, the mechanic, became a car designer according to my grandfather and my cousin the fast food restaurant owner, became the owner of a large chain of restaurants.

Everyone in the village knew he was exaggerating, but it was a like a game, as many of them would also exaggerate about everything.

It always fascinated me, that even though he was ill-tempered and argumentative, he was always popular. People would call out his flaws, but it would generally follow a statement of "at least you always knew where you stood with him."

★

I suddenly started to feel really sad, even though I knew him all my life, I realised that I had never actually known him. All the times I could have got to know him better, I opted to go and ride my bike or play with friends.

A lot of my memories were of him arguing, tormenting my grandmother or drinking with friends. I was sure there was a lot more to him that. Now that he was dead, it was all so final.

Living in London and being so far away from them all, I realised that I was no longer a significant part of their lives anymore. In years to come, would I be the brother that ran away to London that only comes home once a year?

Out of sudden desperation, I was not thinking about the cost of using my mobile phone abroad, I immediately picked up the phone and called my parents. After a number of failed attempts, eventually, my younger brother Asim answered the phone.

"Yes,"

"Hi Asim, it is me, Aziz" I replied,

"What do you want Bro?"

"I just wanted to see how you all are",

"Oh my god, you couldn't have more of a vagina if you tried" he replied.

Chapter Four

Lost Luggage Reclaim

★ ★ ★

During my short conversation with Asim, he had told me that my mother had booked a flight and was currently en route to Cyprus. No sooner had I put the phone down, we made our way to the headquarters of the airline and as it was only a few blocks away, we decided to walk.

While we were walking, I couldn't help notice, my aunt muttering to herself. I tried to listen to what she was saying, but it was hard to hear, as she was speaking quietly. Every so often though, her voice would rise, which would typically involve a swear word or two.

Once we had arrived at the airline headquarters, we were greeted by a sour faced receptionist, far too much makeup and hair tied up tightly, who swiftly told us to take a seat. The headquarters were surprisingly small, and the area we were waiting in was more like a shop than an office. After an hour of waiting, a large man busting out of his suit with food stains all over his shirt came over.

"Don't worry, we have found the luggage, it is now at Ercan Airport."

"Fucking luggage! Are you fucking kidding me?!" It was apparent to everyone that Ayse was no longer in control.

"I meant your father", the man said, even though he had made a mistake, he still made no apology.

We were told to go to Ercan airport to make the final arrangements in relation to transporting the body to its final destination. I thanked the man and took aunt Ayse out of the office as quick as I could, as just by looking at her you could tell that she was liable to get physical with him.

Once we were back in the car, aunt Ayse hardly spoke a word as we drove from Nicosia to Ercan Airport.

"Don't worry aunt, he will be there", but she didn't seem to hear a word of what I said.

"Sorry Aziz, what did you say?"

"He will be there don't worry" I repeated.

"Yes, but how can you misplace a bloody body?!" with that she returned back to her daydream state.

Once we arrived at the airport, I parked the car, and we made our way inside the terminal building. The airport was small, with both the arrivals and departures, though separate, still within the same building. My aunt asked some official looking person near to the entrance about where we should go, he told us to make our way to an office that was on the far side of the airport.

"Fucking lost property! The guy sent us to lost property" she said as she walked towards me, my aunt's concern was now turning into anger. As we made our way to the office, I decided to take over or else this would likely to turn into a blood bath.

"I am looking for my grandfather's body, I was told it had arrived today", I said to the clerk behind the counter.

"What is the name?" it was evident from the way he spoke that the clerk from mainland Turkey.

★

Even before Northern Cyprus became independent from mainland Turkey, there has always been a sort of rivalry between the two countries. Many mainland Turkish people would joke that they hadn't realised that Turks lived on the island and thought only Greeks lived there, which would often be followed by "are you sure you are not Greek?".

Northern Cypriots were just as bad, many of whom, would lord over the fact that they were once part of the commonwealth and had been eligible for UK citizenship.

It wasn't just about identity, the Turkish Cypriot language is also different, the tone and even many of the words are different. Many mainland Turks believe Cypriots have ruined the language, as they don't follow Turkish grammar and also have replaced some Turkish words with Greek and English ones.

"Mustafa Irfan Yangin", I replied

"Yes, he is here, you need to go another office, and they will make the arrangement" with that he pointed us out of his office.

We made our way to the next office, to which the next clerk took us through a number of security checkpoints on our way to where the body had been stored.

The route we were talking enabled us to start seeing the non public areas of the airport. It was a large space with vehicles driving around and suitcases all around us, that had been stored in crates. Every so often you would see a lot of workers sitting and talking.

"No wonder nothing gets done here" my aunt muttered under her breath.

After a short walk, we were taken to a room and in there was a coffin.

"Here is your father."

"I want to see him," my aunt said.

"Of course." With that, the clerk opened the coffin.

"Are you fucking kidding me!" she screamed.

I immediately looked inside. Right in front of us was a large, middle-aged man, who clearly wasn't my grandfather.

★

There was a massive distrust with regards to the airlines that flew into Cyprus. Once when we were returning home from a family holiday, my parents had been asked to identify our luggage from all of the bags spread out on the tarmac before we boarded the flight. My mother could only find two out of the four cases, so she immediately told the airline representative and refused to board the plane until the bags were found.

The airline representative was not happy being ransomed in this way and called the police. The heavily armed police were not amused, and as I had been standing at the base of the stairs, they began ushering me to board the plane. Though the guns were not directly pointing at me, they did, though still have their hands on the guns the whole time.

With every two steps I would take, my mother would shout at me to come back down. To me, my mother was far scarier than any armed police officer, so I just kept on coming back down.

After fifteen minutes, the bags suddenly appeared, and we all boarded the plane. Throughout the whole ordeal my mother was surprisingly calm and once seated and settled within the plane, it was almost as though it had never happened.

By now my aunt could no longer contain herself, so I quickly explained that the body was not my grandfather and that they needed to locate him now.

We were swiftly taken back to the office, and despite the size and scale of the mistake that had been made, none of the clerks made any sort of apology for the error and kept on telling my aunt to calm down. This only made her worse, resulting in her leaving the room four times in the space of fifteen minutes to cool down.

After three separate phone calls, the clerk informed us that my grandfather's body was still in Istanbul and would be arriving at 8 pm that same day.

The clerk told us that he would personally deliver the body and that they would handle all of the paperwork with the government on our behalf.

"Too fucking right you should do this, you are not doing us a favour, you are just doing what you should have done in the first place," my aunt said to the clerk.

As I ushered her out of the door, I thanked the clerk for his help. I actually agreed with my aunt, but I wanted the body to be returned to us and knew that annoying the airline and airport staff would likely cause further delays, so we were operating the good cop, bad cop routine without realising it.

As we drove back to Kyrenia, my aunt was ranting and shouting, I felt it best to not get involved and left her to get it off her chest before we got back to my grandmother.

The main road from Kyrenia to Nicosia goes along the Kyrenia Mountain range. On one side of the mountain, the government had carved into the mountain a large Turkish Cypriot flag, to the annoyance of the Greek Cypriots.

This was typical of Turkish sense of humour and pride, they love to tease and taunt. On the Southern side of the island, tourists would be taken to various viewing points, and the tour guide would inevitably point to the flag, which would then follow a rant relating to his personal view of the war.

By the time we arrived back at the house, my aunt was talking again about her life, so I knew she had calmed down.

"I am really sorry Aziz, but thank you for sorting everything out."

"Don't be silly, let's hope the body arrives soon though" I replied

Once we got back to the house in Kyrenia, I dropped my aunt off and decided to drive onto to the village house. It was a spur of the moment thing, but I felt that the hour long drive by myself was what I needed.

Arriving on the main road in the village, I was struck by how it hadn't changed at all over the years. Despite not having been to Cyprus in years, it had remained as I remembered from my youth. You could have taken a picture in the 1940s, and it would have probably still looked the same. A few more houses scattered around, but pretty much unchanged.

I arrived at my grandparents' house just outside the village and parked up. After spending virtually every summer as a child in Cyprus, I knew all of the streets well.

While I was getting out of the car, a tractor drove past. As it passed, the driver was staring at me intensely. The sight of the tractor made me laugh as I remembered one of our trips to Cyprus.

My cousin Dilan and I were only a few months apart, and of the two of us, he was much more spontaneous, even as a child. Throughout my childhood, he would always talk me into things, resulting in us always getting us into trouble.

While visiting our grandparents, Dilan decided it would be fun for us to drive our grandfather's tractor, without his permission. We were fourteen, and though I told him it was a bad idea, I didn't put up too much of a fight as I also wanted to drive.

After my pathetic attempt of trying to talk Dilan out of it, he went into the house to get the tractor keys. We had picked the perfect time for our plan, our grandmother was at the shops buying groceries, and our grandfather was at the café, probably gambling and arguing.

The tractor was in a shed about a mile away, and we ran all the way in our excitement.

As soon as we entered, Dilan jumped on the tractor and tried to start it up. It was an old tractor and took three attempts before it eventually started. Dilan backed it up, and we were then free to drive around.

Dilan was in his element, going over the little earth mounds and kept on braking hard just to annoy me.

After about twenty minutes, I was getting frustrated and told Dilan it was my turn. Though he complained, eventually he braked hard for the fiftieth time provoking me to hit him and finally pulled over to let me drive.

Once in the driver's seat, I put my foot down hard on the accelerator, I felt so much excitement as the tractor sped up. It was too late by the time I saw the giant ditch on the ground, Dilan was shouting at me to stop, but by the time I did, I was already in the ditch. Immediately, I looked around and was just glad that we were both unharmed.

For some strange reason, once the tractor was in the ditch, I had put my foot back on the accelerator, so the giant wheel of the tractor was spinning fast behind us.

We spent hours trying to get it out, placing wood planks under the wheels, we even tried to get my grandfather's donkey, Ayse, to help. However she was aggressive, and every time we came near her, she would charge at us.

Eventually, we had no choice but to go to the café and tell our grandfather. He swore for at least twenty minutes and began hitting everything except us. Eventually though, he left the café and immediately made his way to the neighbour's house to borrow their tractor, to help pull his tractor out from the ditch.

My grandfather's frustrations seemed to be focused on me the whole time, shouting, as he kept on saying that I should have known better.

We made it worse because my cousin and I couldn't stop laughing whenever he called us 'fucking idiots'; our laughter only made him even angrier.

As I started to walk down the main road, suddenly I heard a loud police siren coming from behind me, as I turned around I saw Adem leaning out of his car with a huge smile on his face.

"Welcome cousin, how are you? Want a lift?" he said.

Many Cypriots believe that when people leave the island to live abroad that two things happen. The first thing they do is put Cyprus in a sort of a time capsule in their mind. The place, as they remember it, stays exactly the same, regardless of when the locals tell them that it is no longer like that, but they still will never believe that their beloved Cyprus has changed.

The second thing is that many get a sort of superiority complex, akin to 'aren't I nice, coming back to see the poor relatives', either way, it annoys the locals no end. I didn't want to come across as either, so I felt it would be rude to refuse.

"I am good thanks Adem and you?" As I climbed into his car, he quickly threw a stash of newspapers and magazines to the backseat, one of which was clearly a porn magazine.

"Where do you want to go?"

"Don't mind" I replied

As we pulled into the centre of the village, there were a lot of cars parked up. For many young Turks, their vehicles are important to them. Many have been modified them to make loud noises or go faster, and given that fuel is so cheap, they are able to drive up and down all day and night showing off to any onlookers.

Once out of the car, I saw a group of old men sitting outside the local cafe. Cafés were common in Cyprus and a place only for men and young boys to socialise, play games and debate the news.

As I got closer, one of the old men, someone well into his eighties got up and came over to offer his condolences.

"Your grandfather was a good person, but loved to argue". A second man joked "He still owes me 20,000 lira".

Before I got to sit down, Adem went inside and came out with a bottle of a local cola. This cola was made in Cyprus and was in all likelihood 90% sugar. It was so sweet that with one bottle you had so much energy you could swim to Lebanon and back.

I sat down looking out on to the street. In the distance, I could see two large men who had just come back from the bakery carrying loaves of bread and other baked goods. As they got closer, it was clear that they both had on clothes that were way too small for them and flip flops.

The clothes were so tiny that both of their stomachs were protruding out from the bottom of their vests and the flip flops that they were wearing sounded like they had given up under the weight of the men. As they got nearer, you could hear one of the men grunting with every step.

As they passed, one of the men suddenly stopped and turned around.

"Aziz, cousin how are you? Do you remember me?"

I hadn't immediately recognised him, but after looking again, I quickly realised it my mother's cousin Emir.

Emir was known by the locals as mad Emir, not because he was insane, more because he was always doing crazy things.

Once Emir had come past our house fast on his motorcycle, which was huge and really loud. Though big, he somehow managed to hide its true size, due to his massive arse and beer belly. He would often be found annoying his neighbours, as he drove this noisy bike up and down the streets of the village, day and night.

On this occasion he came speeding past and upon seeing a snake on the road, he immediately panicked. Not knowing what to do, he steered the bike right and ended up hitting the wall of a house across the street.

Though he was driving fast, he managed to cause no damage. However, the image of this big man's arse, on a motorcycle facing a wall with the back wheel spinning uncontrollably, created amusement for me a for a long time.

"Hi Emir, of course I remember you, how are you?"

"Sorry to hear about your Dede Aziz, you must come to my house".

One of the problems, when you live abroad, is that whenever you visit any country where any of your family are located, you end up spending a lot of time visiting people.

After telling Emir that I would catch-up with him before I left, I looked at my watch. It was getting really late, so I thanked Adem and said goodbye to the men in the café. Adem offered to drive me back to my car, but I insisted that I needed the walk.

✷

There was hardly any traffic on the road back to Kyrenia, and once I had arrived back to the house, it didn't take long for me to realise that more relatives had arrived given the piles of suitcases in the hall.

I went straight into the kitchen to find my mother and aunt sitting there.

"Hi Mum, how are you?"

"Wow, Aziz you have put on weight!" It was ironic as I had only seen my mother just one month before and I was exactly the same weight, but that was typical for my mother, she would be blunt and direct, but everyone was used to it.

"Mum, I tried to call you when I found out about Dede, but no one answered", I said still a bit bemused as to why no one from my immediate family had called me.

"Oh my god Aziz, you are not a kid anymore, we were busy sorting out the flights, that is why we didn't call. Anyway, I told your brother to send you a message, did you not get it."

"No",

"That is typical of Asim, he is so lazy" the moment my mother mentioned my younger brother Asim, it all began to make sense.

"Thanks for going with your aunt, and just so you know, your cousins Dilan and Emir flew with me, and oh, whilst I remember, you will be sharing a room with them."

I didn't relish the idea of sharing a room with my younger cousins, especially as I was in my late twenties and have lived on my own for sometime. Though I was not entirely happy, I knew I had no real choice, so I just said: "Okay mum."

After spending some time catching up with the rest of my family, my cousin Sevda from Australia, whom I hadn't realised had arrived, came running into the room proclaiming

"Dede is here."

Chapter Five

Bed Bath

Once my mother had confirmed that the body was in fact that of our grandfather, my aunt immediately made arrangements for the body to be taken to the village house. When the car left with the body, we all realised it was getting late, and decided to get some rest.

Even though I was exhausted, I didn't end up going to sleep straight away. I hadn't seen Emir and Dilan for well over eight months, so we talked for a couple of hours about what we had all been up to, before falling to sleep.

✷

The next morning I was abruptly woken up by someone shouting "Get up you lazy bastards". I immediately recognised the voice, it was my uncle Ilhan bellowing down the hall.

As I got out of bed, my cousin Dilan, just grunted and pulled the covers over his head in an attempt to go back to sleep.

When I walked into the kitchen, the ritual of breakfast had already commenced, and my grandmother and aunt were already seated.

My mother had decided to keep herself busy and had already started washing the marble floor, however, had quickly discovered that the product she was using had been banned virtually everywhere but Cyprus.

"Mum, do you realise that this product has been banned in the US, given how dangerous it is to your health?"

"It doesn't matter" my grandmother replied, my mother just carried on washing the floor, quickly accepting that her mother really wasn't that bothered.

"Aziz, have you been a good boy for your mummy," asked my uncle Ilhan, as he walked into the kitchen from the garden.

My uncle had just arrived from Germany and had always liked to think himself as a bit of a comedian. Unfortunately, very few people actually found him funny. This short, overweight man, believed that punching you in the arm, was a sign of affection.

Ilhan moved to Germany thirty years ago and seemed to have picked up some of their worst habits. German people are typically very modest, polite people, but they are also known for being somewhat direct at times.

With my uncle, it was almost as if he took the worst from both cultures and become this impolite direct so–called funny man.

"Of course he is Ilhan and stop trying to annoy him," my mother jumped in. She was like kryptonite to my uncle, and he immediately changed the subject.

"Where's dad's body now?" he asked.

"Kerim has taken his body to the village, and everyone will need to go later to prepare Dad" replied my mother.

My mother was the eldest of the eleven children, and though brought up in a very male dominated society, many of her family respected my mother and feared her when she was angry.

There were many stories that her brothers and sisters would reminisce of my mother as a child, it would often involve her being fearless and stubborn, all at the same time.

In Turkish families, you quickly lose count who is family and who is not. Except for my immediate family and first cousins, I have no idea who is who. In Cyprus, you quickly learn that everyone is family and if you ask them, they can easily explain how you are related, even if it the connection is three or four generations back.

Remembering that a number of my family were staying in the house, I quickly ran to one of the bathrooms to have a shower.

A lot of the houses in Northern Cyprus are self-sufficient, with water typically coming from wells, as the piped water would often only come twice a week on specific days, if you were lucky. In addition, many people would also use dual fuel cookers and boilers given that electricity wasn't always the most reliable.

Many of the properties do, however, use a solar panel to heat the water used in the kitchen and bathrooms. If you were unfortunate to be having the third or fourth shower, you were likely to have an icy experience.

After my warm shower, I returned back to my room to get dressed and saw that my two cousins were still asleep. Once dressed, I attempted to wake them up, but with no luck, so I decided that I would leave them sleeping and go back into the kitchen.

"Ilhan will you go with Aziz to the army, he needs to be naturalised" asked my mother. With all the commotion over losing the body, I had completely forgotten about having to be naturalised.

"Maybe, depends if Aziz rubs my foot", with that he exposed his hard skin encrusted foot with one blackened toe. In his youth he had played for the village football team and was supposedly very good, however, two marriages and 5 children later, he was now a short, balding man with more hair on his back than on his head.

"I would rather kiss the donkey" I quickly replied.

"That can be arranged! But of course, I will take you," he said, this time with a sincere look on his face.

"Thank you uncle" I replied

"Thank you for what?", Emir asked as he came into the kitchen.

"It was a thank you for holding your cousin's hand as I have to take him to the big scary army" Ilhan replied.

Though Emir had asked the question, he was clearly not interested in the response as he had already seen the food on the table and had started sawing through the helim.

The phone rang, and as if like lightening my aunt Ayse ran to answer it. It was hard to hear who she was talking to and it was only when she called out to my grandmother that we realised who it was.

"Mum, its Nergis"

"Okay", Nene said, as she slowly rose from her chair, rolling her eyes at the same. Nergis was a close friend of my grandfather. No one was strictly sure what was medically wrong with him, but it looked as if he had no neck and walked like a chicken on heroin.

After a brief conversation, my grandmother thanked him and told him that she would see him later. Before putting down the phone, she said out loud "I can't stand that man, he eats like a pig".

As the receiver was not quite yet down, you could hear a muffled voice from the handset, likely Nergis asking what my grandmother had just said.

My grandmother was oblivious to the fact he was still connected and instead continued to just put the phone back onto the base.

The phone thing was a frequent occurrence with my grandmother, as she never fully understood how the technology worked. She would often talk sweet and softly to the person on the phone, but when she had thought the call was done, would make some sort of remark about the person's behaviour or personality. Luckily for her, most people would just put it down to the fact that she was old.

Nergis had called to say that he had gone to see the priest and all of the arrangements for the funeral within the village had been made. Nergis had always been an excellent friend to my grandfather, and like my grandfather, he had held a senior position in government.

Nergis was the complete opposite to that of my grandfather; where he was quiet and softly spoken, my grandfather was argumentative and often confrontational. Given that they had been friends for such a long time, it seemed like Negris was never put off or phased by his friend's behaviour.

Part of my grandmother's dislike for Nergis was mainly due to one event. On a hot summers evening, my grandfather came home from the local café and proceeded to tell my grandmother to prepare some meat for kofte, as he had invited Nergis around for dinner.

After a short argument around the fact that my grandfather would often invite people round and not give her a lot of notice, she reluctantly prepared the kofte.

Kofte is traditionally lambs mince, skewed onto metal skewers, or flattened into small balls or patties. My grandmother went to work and began rolling the meatballs ready to be barbecued once Nergis arrived.

While the grill was heating up, the two men were happily drinking Raki. My grandfather was so used to drinking the aniseed alcoholic drink that it would take a lot for any real effect to be noticeable.

Once the meat was cooked, a bowl was placed on the table, and as Nergis was the guest, he was handed the bowl to be served first. He quickly began scooping the meatballs from the bowl onto his plate, however also decided that he could no longer wait and put one straight into his mouth from the bowl.

As soon as it entered his mouth, he began making a high-pitched sound. My grandmother looked on through her squinted eyes in disgust as my grandfather struck him on the back. It quickly became evident that the meatball was choking him.

After hitting him a few times, the meatball eventually came hurtling out of his mouth, landing straight back into the bowl.

After Nergis' near death experience, my grandfather decided to take him to the village doctor to get him checked out.

An hour later they returned to the house to resume the meal, only to find that my grandmother, disgusted at the thought of Nergis' regurgitated meatball, decided to throw the entire bowl of meat straight into the bin.

When my grandfather found out what she had done, he was furious, but he soon calmed down, when my grandmother provided them with more Raki, bread and cheese.

My grandmother's lack of technological skills did not just stop with the telephone. Everyone within the family knew to never let her wash your clothes, or else they would come back half the size. Every wash she had ever done was on the highest setting, regardless of the material.

When she got her first microwave, she used it for everything. After nearly blowing up one microwave through putting an entire unopened can inside it, she learnt that the microwave had limitations.

★

With the arrival of another uncle and both cousins having risen, the kitchen was getting very noisy, so I decided to go into the living room for some peace and quiet.

Like a lot of Turkish households, my grandparents had two living rooms; one was for every day use and another that was only ever used for best, for very special visitors. The best living room had green Italian style sofas with wooden trim and ottoman inspired furniture and paintings. As the best living room had a three-seater sofa, I decided to go in there to read the local newspaper.

After laying there for a short while, I started feeling something brush past my neck. Initially, I just flicked whatever it was away with my hand, however after doing this three or four times, I decided to get up to see what was going on.

When I looked back to where I had just been laying, I suddenly saw two or three geckos running in and out of a small hole in the armrest.

Without thinking I let out a loud scream and began jumping up and down, shuddering at the thought of these geckos having been all over me.

It was evident the geckos had made the sofa their home and given the number of them and the strategic holes they had made, they had been living there for some time.

On hearing my screams, my mother and grandmother came rushing in.

"What is wrong Aziz?" my mother asked.

"There are hundreds of geckos in the sofa!"

My mother immediately began laughing, but my grandmother was clearly not amused by my wimpy behaviour and made a sort of tut sound as if to say, man up.

When she looked closely at the sofa and saw the geckos, she had the expression of someone that had seen a turd. She was not amused and rushed out of the room.

She swiftly came back with a broom in hand, and even though she squinted due to her poor eyesight, it seemed that her other senses were supernaturally enhanced.

One by one she whacked the geckos over the head, sometimes taking two or three attempts, but she always got her target in the end.

My mother and I looked on in disbelief as the pile of small geckos started forming.

Once she was content that she had got most of them, she went and got a towel from the kitchen and then placed the fourteen geckos bodies inside the towel and went outside to dispose of them.

Still, in shock at my grandmother's superb aim, we went back into the kitchen. As if nothing had just happened, my mother said: "Right, you and your uncles need to make your way to the village to prepare dad".

Though everyone rolled their eyes, I think they were secretly grateful for the structure and direction she provided.

"I will take mum in the Volvo; Aziz you can drive your aunt and cousins in the Volkswagen". My uncle Ilhan was calculated and had timed his execution well. He knew that transportation would come up and knew that there was no way he was going to drive that old death trap over such a distance.

"Okay, I prefer the Volkswagen anyway, it's retro", I said clearly lying.

"Yeah sure," he said, with a big smirk on his face

My grandfather tended to drive the old Volkswagen more than Volvo, as if trying to preserve the Volvo and keep it in mint condition.

I had bad memories of the Volkswagen. On one holiday, my grandfather decided to drive us to a Famagusta beach one afternoon. My grandparents would love to take us to the beach, but they always had this habit of packing the car as if we were going to move there permanently.

My grandmother would pack in chairs, food, drinks, watermelon, an umbrella, the barbecue and anything else she could find that might useful.

We all piled into the old car and began to make our way to the beach. My grandfather, though a good driver, as he got older, seemed to drive slower and slower. While on the highway, he was clearly annoying all of the other drivers around us by driving at 30 mph on a 70 mph highway.

As the drivers came past, they would typically gesture out of the window and shout abuse at my grandfather. He wouldn't care and would mutter "stupid bastards" as he continued driving as he pleased.

After twenty minutes into the journey, we could all smell burning. After being told by our grandfather that it was all in our imaginations, suddenly smoke started pouring out from the rear of the vehicle. By this point, even my grandfather couldn't deny it any longer.

Once my grandfather had pulled over on the hard shoulder, he told us all to stay in the car. In hindsight, we should have all left the car and ensured we were at a safe distance. We remained in the car as my grandfather had this ability to calm people's nerves, by being seen to be in control.

After fighting with the smoke, he eventually opened the hood of the engine.

"What the hell!" my grandfather began shouting. It had turned out that my grandmother had wedged a huge melon into the shelf above the engine cutting off a number of the air holes that he had created for ventilation. Pressure had built up, which was what was causing the smoke.

Given how much they would always take with them wherever they went, my grandfather had decided to make more room in the car. He did so by building a wooden shelf on top of the engine to store small items and in an attempt to make it safe, had cut small holes all over the shelf to allow the air to circulate within the engine.

Though dangerous, the solution was practical, and up until the melon incident, they never had any previous problems.

After shouting at her, for what seemed like ages, my grandmother had enough and decided she couldn't listen to him anymore. After a brief exchange in Greek, my grandfather threw the watermelon into my lap, and I had to spend the rest of the journey with a huge watermelon between my legs. When we eventually arrived at the beach, I spent the first half an hour walking around bow-legged.

For an old car, it was remarkably resilient, though only ten minutes before there was smoke coming out of the engine, once my grandfather let the car rest and restarted the engine it seemed to work well all the way to the beach.

✱

Once everyone at the house was finished getting ready, we set off to the village, which was an ordeal.

"You drive like an old woman, let me drive", Dilan kept on saying, with my aunt Ayse jumping in with a standard "It's not going to happen Dilan".

Unfortunately for Dilan, he had a bit of a reputation of doing whatever he wanted, whenever he wanted. Everyone knew that if he were to have driven, he would have put his foot down on the pedal and the car would have been screaming all the way to the village, assuming we would have made it there at all.

Because he wasn't seen as responsible, he used to relish at playing the rebel and would just try to wind everyone up.

After an hour and a half, going at a safe 40 mph, we arrived at the house in the village.

As we parked up, uncle Ilhan came over to the car and said "What took you so long", he had a huge smile on his face.

"We stopped off to take a swim in the sea, what do you think??" my aunt Ayse replied.

"You could have, given how long it has taken you."

On seeing our arrival, my mother came over and started ordering everyone around.

"Right the women are going to start getting everything ready, the men need to prepare Dad."

"Prepare him how?" Emir asked

"What do you think Emir! Wash him and prepare him for the funeral" My mother was clearly getting frustrated with her nephew.

"What the....I need to give Granddad a bed bath?" he exclaimed.

Chapter Six

Is That Meant To Be There?

If looks could kill. My mother was not amused and said: "Emir, you know our customs or are you just trying to be awkward?"

Islamic funerals vary from country-to-country, region-to-region, however, it is typical for people of the same sex of the person that has died to wash the body and wrap them in white cotton sheets.

Out of respect, the people that typically wash the body are the immediate family members and close friends, and to be asked is considered to be both a duty and honour.

As we had entered the village house, my mother informed us that my grandfather had been laid out in my grandparent's bedroom, so after my mother had finally finished telling Emir off, we made our way into the room.

Like the rest of the house, the bedroom was dated. The room hadn't changed in all of the years of going to Cyprus, the room had dark wood furniture, marble floors and cotton sheets with embroidered flowers. All around the room were pictures of the entire family from over the years. These pictures were not only in the bedroom, as there were framed photographs of me and other relatives from every year of our lives, scattered all around the house.

We would all laugh whenever we visited, as you would often see embarrassing photographs of each other, photographs you would hope would never get into the wrong hands for fear of being posted on one of those, 'what were they thinking?' websites.

The room was eerie. In the middle was a table where their bed once stood. I was a little taken aback at first. Looking at my grandfather's lifeless body laying there, it looked like he was sleeping and I had never seen my grandfather so quiet before.

Given that he died in London and had to be transported, the funeral home in London helped with the repatriation and had kept my grandfather refrigerated, ensuring that he was laid peacefully. Though he had been stuck in Istanbul Airport, moved from place to place and by now dead for a number of days, he still looked in good condition.

"Hurry up Aziz and help", my uncle Murat said. My second of four uncles had arrived the day before from Dubai. He had much more of a serious personality than that of uncle Ilhan but had little, to no patience. Though I could sense there were other people in the room, I was so fixated on my grandfather that I hadn't noticed him at the top of the table.

Growing up, I rarely ever saw uncle Murat. He was the eldest uncle but was now more Middle Eastern than the rest of the family. He had married a woman from the United Arab Emirates and made his life there. He was a teacher, however for my family, he was more like the Arab enforcer. If I called him on my birthday to thank him for the gifts he had sent, he would go into a rant about our customs and what it means to be an Arab.

Helping with the cleansing of my grandfather's body were my four uncles Murat, Ilhan, Naim and Osman; my two cousins Dilan and Emir and myself. More family members had arrived in Cyprus, but it was my grandmother's wish that her sons and three eldest grandsons would wash her husband.

Before I had come into the room, my family had already started the ritual, and a white cotton sheet known as Auwra had been placed from my grandfather's belly button down to his knees. The purpose of this part of the ritual was to ensure that the privacy of the deceased remains intact.

"What should I do? I asked. My uncle Naim threw over a cloth and a pair of gloves and said: "Wash, what do you think?"

Uncle Naim was the second eldest and like his brother Murat had no sense of humour. When we were eight, my cousin Dilan and I decided it would be funny to put a small bottle of milk underneath the seat of his car, hidden from view.

As the weeks went past, the milk went sour and the smell got worse, he kept on cleaning the car, spraying a variety of products, but nothing worked, it was only after 4 weeks when the smell was so unbearable that he pulled the car apart and found the bottle.

The smell was like rotten eggs and colleagues and friends would refuse lifts from my uncle, given how bad the smell was.

Though it started off as a joke, both my cousin and I, ended up being too scared to inform him of the bottle, or even later on, to admit it was us that had placed it there. He was so angry and kept on saying what he would do if he ever found out who had done it.

Even though Ilhan saw himself as the joker and at least tried to be funny, all of my mother's brothers were far too serious and often extremely moody. It was a trait that ran all through the entire family, the 'serious and not able to take a joke gene'.

The body lay on the table and at each section of my grandfather's body was a family member washing. All the time we were cleaning with water, and when the process started, each member of the family said "In the name of Allah". Outside the room, we could hear people around the house crying.

"Will someone tell them to stop", said uncle Osman, who was clearly getting irritated by the younger members of the family wailing in the adjacent rooms.

"They are just upset uncle", as the words left my mouth, my uncle gave me a cutting look.

"We are all upset Aziz, but this is not how it is meant to be" he replied.

I knew he was right, but though my grandparents were religious, many of the grandchildren were not and as most had grown up in the USA and Australia, were more accustomed to seeing Christian style funerals, where people would cry and show their grief.

Uncle Murat handed me a handful of new lotus leaves and told me to continue cleaning. The ritual of washing the body of the deceased it to wipe away any impurities. Watching my uncles and cousins, who all like to act macho, being so gentle and tender with my grandfather's body, was slightly strange.

They were all clearly upset, and from the look on their faces, you could tell they were thinking "Don't cry, don't cry", as to cry in front of any of the others, was a big no-no, so they just kept their heads down and prayed.

After gently wiping my grandfather's arms and chest, there was a sweet smell in the air; a mixture of my uncles and cousins' aftershave and the sweet smell from the lotus leaves that were now beginning to pile up in the corner of the room. We repeated this ritual four times, and with each time, we would use new gloves, cloths and lotus leaves.

I couldn't help but keep looking at my grandfather's serene face. In life, he was such a strong man, so opinionated and fearless.

Like my grandmother, he was often known to talk about people. However, the difference with my grandfather was that he had no problem telling the person to their face, what he actually thought of them.

✮

As a youngster coming to Cyprus, we would often go to the café with our grandfather. He would sit outside with friends, while we stayed inside playing pool or video games.

Every so often you would hear shouting outside, it was usually because of a game they played called Tavla, a Turkish version of backgammon. Although I have played it hundreds of times, the rules always seemed to change depending on who I was playing with.

I went outside to see what was going on and found my grandfather sitting, well almost crouching, on a small stool, with a small table in-between him and an old friend of my grandfathers.

My grandfather jumped up and threw the table in the air. "You fucking cheater" he shouted. He had clearly been playing for money, and his friend had won.

"You are such as bad loser Bull". A lot of my grandfather's friends called him 'the Bull', as he would go into things head first and was known by them to have a really quick temper.

My grandfather lunged at his friend, but before I could act to stop the fight, two elderly men jumped in to pull them apart.

Watching them was like watching two young men in the locker room fighting after a football match, not two old pensioners.

"I will cut out your tongue out you liar", my grandfather said, with his fist flying around. It was all show as the two men were too far apart to even attempt to fight one another at this stage.

After a short while, once things had calmed down, I went over and asked my grandfather if he was okay, he just replied: "mind your business".

I decided to go back in and play pool. I went back outside an hour later, and my grandfather and the friend he had just fought with, were now laughing and drinking Turkish coffee.

★

At the last part of the ritual, everyone went a little slower as they knew the ceremony was coming to an end and wanted to take the time to remember my grandfather for the last time.

The cleaning ritual must be performed by an odd number of people, and once the final washing had taken place, my uncles began drying my grandfather's body with clean towels. Once dried they covered the body with the first white cotton sheet; all of the sheets used were plain, simple and inexpensive cotton.

The next part of the process is called the shrouding, which consists of wrapping the body in three white sheets. Once the shrouding was completed, my grandfather's body lay there wrapped in white cotton sheets, and although we knew it was my grandfather, you could no longer see any part of his body or face.

At this point, the local priest walked into the room to perform the funeral prayer for us. The priest Ozturk was my grandmother's first cousin. He was short like my grandmother and had a long beard.

Notwithstanding that he was a priest, Ozturk had a presence about him. Though first cousins, my grandmother and Ozturk rarely saw each other and many in the village would be very critical of him, for he did not always observe all of the Islamic teachings. He actually was a bit of rebel, and when confronted he would say "I follow my understanding of the teachings."

You would often see him having a cigarette by the entrance to the mosque. Though Northern Cyprus and Turkey are Muslims, the interpretation of the Koran, its teachings and devotion can sometimes vary region-by-region.

On one trip in my youth, I decided that I wanted to take some photographs of the village to show my mother and other relatives back in the US. I was staying with my grandparents in their village house and so I decided to venture out on my own.

Happily minding my business and taking the pictures, not even ten minutes had passed when a police car pulled up alongside me. The police officer immediately started shouting, asking what I was doing.

It seemed that someone in the village had seen me taking photographs and had called the police for fear that I was a Greek spy taking pictures of the surrounding Greek homes. At that time, there was a lot of suspicion by locals of a Greek conspiracy.

Ever since the war, it was believed that some Greek Cypriots would ask visitors to take photographs of their old land, houses and even the churches. Many people had been apprehended, typically tourists, who had done so innocently believing what harm would be caused by taking a few photographs.

My grandfather was a regular visitor to a number of the police stations in the region, to act as translator and to assist in helping to free the often shocked and frightened tourists.

Whenever he would come home after helping someone that had just been released, he would say "Bloody paranoid police". He knew, like a lot of people, that it was only natural for people to be intrigued as to the state and condition of their previous homes and it wasn't like the tourists were taking pictures of army bases or ones relating to the country's defences.

The moment I said my full name, I could see the look of horror on the face of the police officer. My grandfather was well known all over Northern Cyprus, so typically people knew that if they did anything to his family, without good reason, they were likely to have a problem with my grandfather.

The policeman swiftly apologised and drove off to the house that had clearly called in claiming that I was some sort of spy. I continued taking photographs, but when I returned back to the village house, I told my grandmother what had happened and she was not amused. She wanted me to tell her the house that had called it in, as she wanted to go confront them. I brushed it off to avoid all the drama.

As it was getting dark, I remembered that I hadn't taken a photograph of my great grandfather's house, which was in the old part of the village. So as not to disappoint my mother, I decided I would venture back out.

When I told my grandmother that I was going out to take more photographs, she insisted on coming with me. Knowing my grandmother, she wanted to be there if there was a repeat of what happened earlier.

The sun was going down, and as we walked into the village, every house we walked past my grandmother began telling me about the people that lived there; "This house the husband cheated with the next door neighbour; this house their son is living with a man".

As we got closer to the old part of town, I began taking pictures, and as it was still light enough, the flash wasn't going off. I turned around and noticed that just behind the mosque that the sun was going down, it was the perfect shot. I was too far away to take the picture properly, so I told my grandmother that I needed to get closer.

The window of the mosque was open, and I could see that inside some worshippers were being led in prayer by the priest Ozturk. I crept passed the window, lined up and took the picture.

Suddenly the flash went off alerting the worshippers through the window, and you could hear them getting angry as they made their way to the door. Though there is no rule around taking pictures of mosques, it is considered rude to take them when people are in prayer.

My grandmother and I quickly left the scene undetected, by now she was laughing uncontrollably like a young girl getting up to mischief. Whenever my grandmother laughed it was so infectious, you couldn't help but laugh with her.

We both were making each other laugh, and by the time we got back to the house, we both were in pain from laughing.

Now that my grandfather's body was all prepared, my uncle Murat pulled out a large Turkish flag. The flag had actually belonged to my grandfather, and I remembered it only too well.

My grandfather like his friend Nergis, was a government official before he retired and throughout his career, he held senior positions in various government departments.

As a former area representative and government employee, my grandfather would oversee any official funerals in the region.

Part of my grandfather's responsibility was to drape the flag over the deceased person's body. When the body would be laid in the ground, the flag would be removed.

When I was 10 and visiting my grandparents, I woke up one morning, walked into the kitchen and suddenly saw this flag all folded up on the minder.

Tempting a 10-year-old with something that looked like a cape and with colours that resembled something that superheroes would wear, was too much for me to bear. I draped the cape around my neck and began running around the house, watching the cape fly behind me.

The faster I ran, the more the cape would lift up. I was 'Super Turk', saving the people from anyone that would seek to harm them.

When my grandfather returned back from the café, he walked into the living room to discover me in my superhero get up. As soon as he saw me, he began shouting "take it off now, you stupid boy". I was defiant and ran into my bedroom and closed the door.

In all of the commotion, I hadn't actually realised that my mother and grandmother were sitting outside in the shade and once my grandfather went outside to speak to my mother, she came running in.

She burst open the door, dragged the cape from me and took me straight into the bathroom. She told me to undress and have a shower straight away.

Once I was cleaned, and in new clothes, my grandfather explained that it wasn't a cape and that it had been used to bury countless people.

After screaming for about ten minutes, I finally calmed down, and for days after I became fixated on my cleanliness. It had taken at least a week before I felt clean again.

As the flag was draped over my grandfather, my cousin Emir gasped in horror.

"Oh no! I am so sorry, I think I left one of the cloths in-between the sheets, during the shrouding."

I looked around, and the colour had drained from the faces of each of my uncles, coupled with a look of pure horror.

"Only kidding! I am just trying to lighten the mood," Emir said after a pause.

Uncle Murat slapped Emir across the face and snarled "Show some fucking respect".

Chapter Seven

Too Shiny

✵ ✵ ✵

Once the shrouding ceremony had ended, I left the bedroom and made my way to the living room. On my way, I was trying to work out who was able to come over to Cyprus for the funeral at such short notice. With ten aunts and uncles and over thirty cousins, I knew not all of them would be able to make it over in time.

Several of my female cousins were sitting on the living room floor, rocking and crying. Amongst them was my cousin Sevda. Sevda's mother was one of my mother's younger sisters who lived in Australia.

Sevda's speedy arrival to the funeral was more coincidence than planning. Sevda and her sister Azra were both in their twenties, and Sevda was getting to the age where she was desperate to get married to a good Turkish boy.

The problem for Sevda and her family was that they lived in Western Australian and unfortunately for the girls, there wasn't an abundance of eligible Turks in the local community.

Her father, who was from a village on the other side of the island decided to take direct action and bring the girls to Cyprus for a four-week holiday, to see if they could find potential suitors.

Any prospective suitors were strictly vetted and quizzed to ensure that they would be happy moving and making a new life in Australia, with one of my aunt's precious daughters.

Azra was more a natural beauty of the two, but as my family were quite traditional, Sevda, being the eldest, had to be married first.

Even in Cyprus, Azra was getting a lot of interest, whilst Sevda was being treated by many suitors' families as the second place prize.

The problem with Sevda was that she was so desperate to get married and start a family. Whereas western culture had rubbed off on Azra, who actually wasn't interested in marrying a man from the village and secretly wanted a blonde-haired surfer dude.

Sevda had men interested, however not ones that met her criteria. Back in Australia, there was a boy in the local neighbourhood, who was about the same age as Sevda. The young Australian boy was obsessed with her, but unfortunately for him, he did not meet the first of Sevda's criteria; he wasn't Turkish.

Though many Turks over the years have married people from other nations, Turkish people are very nationalist, and there is a preference by many of them to marry within their own community.

Sevda's desperation to get married, also made any potential suitors worry as to what was wrong with her and why she was still unmarried, causing a catch-22 situation for her. It didn't also help that any would-be suitors would have to move halfway across the world and start a new life in Australia.

"Aziz are you okay? Is it done?" I could see that Sevda had been crying for some time, her eyes were bloodshot, and the skin around her eyes was extremely puffy. I wasn't sure if it was grief or just all the rushing around, but I couldn't help but notice that her hair was all over the place and she had stains on her clothes.

"It is done, I just need to go get cleaned up" I replied.

Now that my grandfather was prepared, all of the men had to go wash and get ready to go to the mosque. The women are not allowed to go to the mosque or to be inside the cemetery during the burial, but there is an area in which they are able to see the funeral from afar.

Given that seven of us needed to get ready, two of my uncles went to the house next door, which belongs to one of my grandfather's first cousins.

The other two uncles went to a great aunt's house in the village, and my mother had arranged for my two cousins and I to go and get washed at the home of one of her close childhood friends.

We left the house and made our way to get cleaned, I walked ahead of Dilan and Emir as they were both messing around, trying to push the other over, not seeming to care that we were meant to be in mourning.

"Welcome, my sincere condolences," said my mother's friend Aydin, as she opened the door.

Aydin had been a friend of my mother since her school days; a friend that, even though they lived halfway around the world from each other, would speak at least once a week and my mother had always considered her as part of the family.

Unfortunately, like so many villages, gossip about people was rife, and Aydin had a number of rumours spread about her. Before we entered the house, Dilan and Emir hung back and were whispering to themselves.

"Thank you so much aunt for letting us get ready in your home," I said I entered. Dilan pushed passed me at the door, as he passed I hit him in the arm and told him for him to stop whispering with his brother.

Aydin had married young, it had been arranged and unfortunately was not a happy marriage. Aydin's husband liked to drink and would often drink to excess and come home and take it out on Aydin. The morning after, he would often claim that he did not know what he was doing and apologise for his behaviour.

On one particular occasion, her husband went too far and beat her badly, so badly, that she became fearful for her life.

Aydin's husband had been drinking since lunchtime on this particular day, and by the time he got home he was really drunk. Aydin had made dinner, but he quickly became enraged by what she had prepared. He proceeded to grab Aydin by the head and pushed her face into his plate of food.

She tried to fight back, but he was a big man and very strong. He worked as a farmer and spent all day lifting and digging. Given that Aydin was fighting back, he began to slap and punch her hard, in an attempt to control her.

She could feel the blood running down her face, but her survival mode kicked in, and when she had the opportunity she fell to the floor and kicked her husband's legs hard. The pressure forced him to fall back, giving Aydin the chance to flee the house.

Aydin left and ran to a neighbours' house where she called her brother to collect her. Her brother arrived, took her to her parents' house and unknown to Aydin, returned to confront her husband.

After a lot of arguing with his brother-in-law, Aydin's brother even more enraged by his brother-in-law's lack of respect for his sister and for the lack of remorse he displayed, couldn't take it anymore. While arguing he saw a glass bottle of 7up sitting on the table. He picked up the bottle, wrestled his brother-in-law to the ground and rammed the glass bottle deep into his brother-in-law's arse.

By the time the police had arrived, Aydin's brother was described as calm and looking happy. The brother-in-law though was not doing so well. There was blood all over him as the bottle had shattered upon entry.

Aydin's brother was sent to prison for two years, and the brother-in-law, not only had to recover from his injuries he had received, but also from the beating the police officers had given him once they discovered what he had been doing.

After recovering, Aydin's husband tried to reconcile with her, but Aydin refused to take him back. Throughout the village, people would frequently joke that her husband never walked or sat down the same way ever again.

On one trip out when I was sixteen years old, I met Aydin's brother. By now he had served his time, and during one of our meetings, I asked if he regretted doing it.

He just replied, "I only regret being caught, but I would do it a thousand times again for my sister".

As Aydin lead us into the kitchen, she asked: "Would you boys like a drink?"

"Do you have 7up?" said Dilan as he burst out laughing.

I was so angry with my cousins that I immediately told them to go outside, and as they left they were both still giggling loudly. They wouldn't be giggling if my mother heard of this disrespect.

"I am so sorry aunt for my stupid cousins."

"It is okay Aziz, I am used to it by now" she replied. You could see from Aydin's face that this was a normal thing for her to have to face.

"Don't worry about idiots like them, they need to grow up" I replied.

Aydin was in her early fifties and was still an attractive woman. Many men had tried to get her attention over the years, however according to my mother, the experience with her husband had left her wanting to be alone and made her self-reliant.

Many Turkish women go from being protected and sheltered by their families, to being married and having to be responsible for a whole new family of their own, with very little preparation.

For many, they are young and inexperienced and also have to deal with a domineering mother-in-law who believes their precious son can do no wrong. It can take them years, if ever, to find their feet and be in control.

Arranged marriages were still commonplace, however, given that Cyprus is made up of small communities, families typically show interest, and it is for both the girl and her parents to choose who the preferred groom would be. It is not as archaic as it once was, and although the potential suitors are still chaperoned as they get to know one another, the decision is now made mutually.

It still doesn't take away from the fact that you have two relative strangers making a lifelong decision, at typically a young age.

Once my cousins had regained their composure, I let them back into the house and made them apologise to Aydin. Once they had apologised, Aydin took us up to one of the bedrooms and provided us with towels.

✶

While we were getting ready Emir asked "Do you think Nene, will stay in Cyprus now?". To be honest, I hadn't thought of it until he mentioned it.

None of my grandmother's children or grandchildren lived in Cyprus, so with her husband now dead, I wasn't sure what was going to happen.

"I reckon she is going to live with your mum Aziz" Dilan responded.

This was not unheard of in Cyprus. Many children migrated away from Cyprus over the years, and it wasn't unheard of for large families to only have the elderly parents or grandparents still living in Cyprus.

Turkish families are extremely close, and even distance doesn't change that. With sisters and brothers half way around the world, my mother would speak to them for hours on the telephone. Every month when the phone bill would arrive, my father would look it at in disgust, but would never say anything, as he knew how important family was to my mother.

It was rare for Turkish families to put relatives into care homes. The children are taught to always take responsibility for the elderly members of the family, regardless of how annoying they might be.

For older people where they had no family living in Cyprus, neighbours or distant relatives would step in and help with the care. Right or wrong the community looked after one another.

"The only problem is, that she hates LA, I can imagine her walking down the strip insulting poor unsuspecting celebrities, telling them what she thinks of them" I replied.

My grandmother had visited LA a few times over the years and with each visit her face would always give away what she was actually thinking. She would often squint with a grimacing look on her face as skimpily dressed young girls and men dressed in pastel colours walked past.

"I am sure my mother wouldn't mind though", I said.

After having my shower, I quickly finished getting ready. Both Dilan and Emir were still messing around and took twice as long as they should getting ready. Once ready, we made our way downstairs.

"Thank you so much aunt for letting us use your home."

"Not at all Aziz, tell your mother that I will speak to her tomorrow, again please pass on my condolences to the rest of your family". With that Aydin kissed us all in turn on the cheek as we left her home.

"She is alright, I don't think she is a lesbian" said Dilan as we headed back to the house.

"Who told you she was a lesbian?" I asked.

"People in the village said that was part of the reason why her husband would beat her because she didn't like men."

"That is absolute rubbish", I replied.

This is typical in small communities. It was evident that Aydin's husband, who was embarrassed at the fact his wife wouldn't take him back, would rather discredit her than take accountability for the fact he was abusive to her for years.

After rejecting him a number of times, he actually moved on and married someone else, but unfortunately, my mother told me that many in the village had seen his new wife with bruises on her arms, so I guess the 7up episode didn't really teach him a lesson.

I didn't want my cousins to continue with all the rumours about this poor woman, so I changed the subject.

"So Dilan, do you have a girlfriend now?"

"Kind of," Dilan said evasively

"What do you mean kind of?"

"Well there are a few girls that think we are dating, but I kind of don't" he responded, with a massive grin on his face.

Dilan and Emir were brothers and both really tall, like most of the men in our family. Dilan was the lighter skinned of the two, with light brown hair and bright green eyes, while Emir had jet black hair and brown eyes which complimented his slightly darker skin.

Dilan was now 27 years old, and incredibly lazy. To date, the most notable thing he had ever done, was to have finished high school. As Dilan was the eldest of the two brothers, he had a strange relationship with his parents, with his mother openly spoiling him. When he turned 16, his mother bought him a brand-new car. When he turned 21, his mother bought him an apartment; he was clearly the favourite child and knew it.

Though Dilan was really immature, he was well liked. He had a charm about him, and coupled with his looks, he could get people to do anything for him; women would queue up, even when they knew what he was like.

Emir was the opposite, he was now 23 and currently studying for a masters degree in finance. He had a geeky, cheeky charm about him and though popular with women, he had been with the same girl since high school.

He was kind of mature most of the time, but whenever he was together with his older brother, it was like they both went back in time, back to when they were teenagers.

Since Dilan had moved out from the family home, the two brothers spent less time together. However, Emir would often go around to his brother's apartment just to hang out.

"What about you Aziz?" I could tell that my cousin was apprehensive about asking.

*

Dilan's apprehension was due to an event two years prior. I was ready to marry my fiancé Ayla. We had been together since high school, and she had been the love of my life.

We had planned to start a big family and have a huge Turkish wedding, but on the day of our wedding, she got cold feet and left me to go and volunteer in Africa for six months. I was devastated at the time. Although I understood that the pressure of the wedding had gotten to her, what had upset me more, was that she had never actually spoken to me about her concerns. Running away, the way she did, just left me confused and having to face everyone to explain what had happened.

It was old news now, but I re-evaluated my whole life as a result of what had happened and decided to leave Los Angeles to start a new life in London.

"Actually there is a girl at work, but it is casual, nothing too serious" I replied.

"Please tell me she is Turkish, Mummy would not approve", Dilan said taunting and teasing.

"Actually she is Italian, and I don't care what anyone thinks", my words came out a bit more aggressive than I meant them to be.

"Oh listen to him"Dilan mocked.

Two of my uncles were standing outside grandmother's house when we arrived

"What is going on?" I said

"Your great-uncle Irfan has arrived with his family", uncle Murat said, not looking amused.

My great uncle Irfan was the brother of my grandfather, and they had not spoken for over 40 years due to a disagreement over the wedding of his daughter.

My grandfather had lent his brother Irfan some money to pay for the wedding, and to my grandfather's annoyance, his brother acted like it never happened.

My grandfather never one for letting things go, went around telling everyone in the village what a crook his brother was, which only fuelled the argument.

Shortly after the wedding, my grandfather and his brother had a massive argument, and both families never spoke to one another again. The irony was that great uncle Irfan lived only ten houses down from the village house, however, should they have seen each other, it was like they were looking at an empty space.

Most Turkish families are hot blooded and with that comes feuds and arguments, but the one thing that makes them reconcile is death. It is strange how they are happy to do in death, what they could not do in life.

When I walked into the living room, great uncle Irfan came over and hugged me.

"Do you remember me, I am your uncle Irfan?" he asked. It actually was incredibly awkward, as I knew who he was, but had never actually met or spoken to him in my lifetime.

"Of course uncle, thank you for coming", with that he kissed me on both cheeks. It was strange to look at him, as he looked so similar to my grandfather, you could clearly see they were brothers.

"I miss Mustafa so much" uncle Irfan said. As soon as the words were spoken, everyone in the room began looking at each other. Though I am sure, they were close when they were younger, to miss someone that you haven't spoken to for decades is somewhat pushing belief.

Right as he had said it, my mother walked into the living room, clearly ignoring what she had just heard.

"Aziz, you took your time, at least you look clean now; did you use face cream or something as your face is looking way too shiny?"

Chapter Eight

Two Large To Fall

★ ★ ★

Grievers continued to turn up at the house to pay their respects to my family. Once inside, all eyes were on my grandmother, though she was sat there quietly, she was getting visibly irritated at having so many people in her home.

I watched my grandmother staring at two young boys playing with toy cars on her marble floors. She was somehow managing to speak to well-wishers and at the same time staring at the kids to ensure that her floors remained intact. Quite a feat, being able to have one eye on one person and the other on something else.

My grandmother and mother, like most of the Turkish people I have met in my lifetime, are extremely hospitable and generous. Growing up, my mother would typically cook meals for ten people, when actually there were only five of us in the family. We knew never to question it, as the answer would always be the same "What if someone were to turn up?"

Unfortunately for me, on the days when no one turned up, I would end up eating two or three portions, which resulted in a childhood of obesity and constant taunting by my family. This scenario plays out in a lot of Turkish families as food is associated with joy and togetherness, however, although you are encouraged to eat, when you lack self-control as I did, you are then ridiculed for your inability to stop yourself after the third plate of food.

I would always be the first to be questioned over any food that had gone missing, and although most of the time it was me that had eaten it, I am sure there were times when my siblings would let me take the blame for the occasional missing chocolate bar or bag of crisps.

Hospitality, when it came to food and drink, was not a class thing, more an ingrained social behaviour, no matter how rich or poor, you would offer your guests whatever you had available to you.

I decided to get outside for some fresh air and knew that I would have to make my way to the mosque at some point, so thought I decided to walk there a little earlier, rather than just sitting outside trying to avoid the well-wishers.

As I got closer to the mosque, I could see a group of men all standing near to the entrance. As I got closer, I immediately recognised my mother's cousin Emir.

"How are you cousin?" Emir said.

"I am okay thank you", I replied.

He then began to introduce me to the other men standing outside of the mosque. I had recognised two of them, and during the introduction, I found out that the other men were yet another Mustafa, Ali, Ahmed or Hussein that all were related to us in some way.

The two men I had immediately recognised were first cousins of my mother; Hussein, who was also known as 'the moaner' and Serdar, also known as 'man-girl'. Nicknames like the moaner and man-girl were common in the village and were typically said in a joking way. However once labelled, it was hard for people to lose these given nicknames. A change of nickname only really occurred when someone did something more extreme or much funnier, to warrant a new nickname.

The moaner was related to my mother through her father's side and had one feature that dominated his entire face; an enormous bulging nose. It was so big that all you saw was the nose, and you had to really focus your attention to see any of his other features.

I recall the first time I had met Hussein. I was with my cousin Dilan, and upon seeing him, Dilan remarked about his nose. Hussein tried to joke around, replied "big nose, big…" Being only six at the time it took me years to actually know what he meant, as my mother refused to answer the endless "What did he mean?" questions from me.

Hussein was a successful man, owned a number of businesses and had a wife and three daughters, all of whom were beautiful. Even with successful businesses and a loving family, Hussein was never happy.

If you said to him what a lovely day it was, he would reply that it will probably rain. If you told him that you had no money, he would say that he too was struggling financially. Clearly a lie, but he wasn't going to be outdone by anyone. Hussein was such a moaner that he would often lie, just to get the upper hand, as if it were a competition to have it worse than anyone else.

Most people avoided him as much as they could, for he was like a dark cloud wherever he went and too much exposure would result in you walking away feeling depressed. Countless times I saw people's enthusiasm turn into negativity at the hand of Hussein. On one occasion at the café, one of the old men was happy that his daughter-in-law was pregnant and that it was going to be a boy.

"Can they afford to have a child? I heard his job doesn't pay that well" Hussein queried.

The other man, Serdar was the village mechanic and was related to my mother through marriage, as he had married her first cousin Fatima.

His nickname, 'man-girl' was given to him by his fellow villagers and friends as he displayed a few mild feminine mannerisms. He would often use his hands when he spoke, and his voice was a little higher than most. You might assume with a nickname like that he would be somewhat camp, but Serdar was a man's man, albeit rather expressive with his hands.

Many Cypriots being the way they were, picked up on this and turned his behaviour into a nickname.

Serdar was in his late thirties, happily married and was yet to have children. Naturally, the gossips loved to talk: "maybe they don't have sex and just cuddle all night", and "maybe his wife doesn't have all the parts he wants."

Though Serdar knew people were talking about him, he always came across as someone that didn't really care about what was being said of him, an attribute that I really admired about him.

The gossiping stopped for a while when one man in the café got a bit too drunk on Raki and insulted Serdar's wife. Within seconds the man, close to Serdar's age, was on the floor with Serdar punching him hard. After a while, the onlookers in the café must have got bored with the show and decided to pull them apart.

This display of aggression in defence of his wife didn't go unnoticed, and for a while, people were wary of Serdar, and his nickname became something that was said behind his back and not to his face.

Even though they gave him a cruel nickname, he was one of the best mechanics in the village and given his talents and personality, there was a lot of respect for him.

On one of my younger fatter holidays to Cyprus, I recall asking my mother why were people so cruel. Though no one had actually said anything to me, you can tell what a Turk thinks, simply by looking at the face. I used to get the looks that said 'that kid needs to get some exercise' or 'his mother needs to learn to say no to that fat kid.'

As soon as I asked the question, I immediately regretted it. However on this occasion, she had responded in an unfamiliar way, "People say these things for two reasons, yes to tease and taunt, but also out of love", and she went on to elaborate.

"Okay Aziz, you are fat. Imagine going to school, where every day at home I tell you are not fat and look perfect."

I was surprised to hear her even saying the word perfect as she only ever used it in the context of when she talking about babies. It didn't matter if she knew the family or not, she was often found in shopping malls speaking and pinching the cheek of babies, while a confused mother looked on trying to work out how to respond.

"Then imagine the children at school teased you for being fat, do you think it would hurt if you hadn't heard it before?"

"Well, I guess" I replied.

"People looking in may see it as cruel, but it is said out of love to protect and disarm anyone that may want to use something against the people we love".

Strangely it made sense. As a child I knew I was fat so if someone said anything I had the attitude "And what? You are..."

This defence mechanism served many Turkish children well growing up in foreign countries, especially given how funny some Turkish names sound to western ears.

That being said, even though some of the nicknames could be cruel, I never saw any real malice behind them. Although used in a taunting way, friends would spring to the defence against those who weren't part of the family or village and had no right to use the name.

★

Just outside the mosque, we performed the ablutions, a cleansing ritual. Once completed, I entered the mosque and as I walked in, I saw that there were people already inside. Two of my uncles were there, along with some old men that were close friends and relatives to my grandfather.

Everyone that entered the mosque did it quietly and immediately pulled out their prayer mats and ensured they were facing towards Mecca. Once everyone had arrived the priest, Ozturk began the prayer. The mosque was small, but very clean and there was a fresh smell of jasmine in the air. A breeze was coming from the windows, alongside each were large fans blowing so hard that it would have been hard to hear, had it not been for the loudspeakers and the priest speaking through a microphone.

Mosques outside of prayer are generally very peaceful places. This particular mosque had an enormous domed ceiling and a tall turret, known as a minaret. The minaret had a tall spire that towered over the village. At the top, the speakers were strategically placed around the onion shaped crown. These speakers were used by the priest to call worshippers to prayer five times a day. This call to worship is also known as Ezan.

The prayer times varied by time zone and season, but typically the first would be at sunrise, and the last would be close to sunset around 6 pm.

As a child, I would listen out for the call to prayer as it was a confirmation that I was back in Cyprus.

I looked around at all of the people in the mosque that had come there specifically for my grandfather. There was a lot of my extended family, but there was also a significant number of close friends of my grandfather.

There was a sweet smell in the air. Although everyone performed their ablutions, when I was younger I would always be fearful of smelly feet, given that everyone inside the mosque was bare footed.

This started after a trip to the blue mosque in Istanbul with my family. Before we entered the mosque, we all washed. However, there were hordes of tourists already inside and more still queueing up outside. Although they had taken off their shoes in respect, the summer months are sweltering in Istanbul, so by the time they had arrived at the mosque they had built up a sweat; that sweat transferred to the carpets that lined the floors to make an awful smell of sweaty feet.

I asked one of the guides within the mosque why they didn't use one of the carpet freshener products to get rid of the smell, in which he just pretended he hadn't heard me and my mother hit my arm and told me to shut up.

On that same trip though, at another mosque, I was getting a little bored of the guide, so I started to look around to find questions to ask to annoy him.

"Why are there no cobwebs on the ceiling?" I had looked around, and the ceilings were huge with not a single cobweb; my mother gave me a dirty look, but the guide seemed surprised that I had asked.

"That is a great question! Mosques typically paint ostrich eggs black and string them to the ceilings. These blackened eggs scare away spiders and stop them from forming webs."

Though my question was meant to annoy, everyone in the group was impressed, and as soon as we returned home to the US, my mother immediately began painting her newly purchased ostrich eggs.

Once the prayer had finished, my four uncles lifted up my grandfather's body, and we all made our way to the cemetery, which was just outside the village. Everyone was quiet as they left the mosque.

All of the male members of the family entered the cemetery while all of the women, including my grandmother, were standing and observing the funeral from afar. Looking back at them all, though a significant number of them were crying, there was very little noise, like they were holding in any sound.

A grave had been dug, and my uncles placed my grandfather's body on his right-hand-side into the ground, ensuring that his head was facing towards Mecca. The whole time, there were reciting "In the name of Allah and in the faith of the Messenger of Allah".

Once the body was inside the grave, a layer of stones was placed on top of the body, as in Muslim burials there should be no direct contact between the body and soil when the grave it filled.

★

Looking back at the women, I noticed that my mother was standing in between her two sisters, consoling them. My mother was of average height, but had a slim build, unlike the two sisters, that she was consoling.

Both aunts were from America, and they loved the fast food culture of the US way too much. Their body shape was considered more square than apple or pear.

Aunt Lale was the mother of Dilan and Emir and was the aunt I was closest to growing up. Like my family, Lale, her husband Hussein and four children grew up in Los Angeles about a fifteen-minute drive away from our house.

My aunt Lale used to be a teacher, but when she hit 50, she came home from work and told her husband that she didn't want to work anymore. She now spends her life having coffee mornings with her friends, gossiping and the majority of the time eating.

Aunt Lale wasn't a massive fan of actual food, it was all about sweet syrupy desserts for her. You could go to her house any time of day, and you would find a collection in her fridge. Whenever we visited, our mother would lay down the rules, no more than one sweet and you have to eat proper food.

My mother's other sister Mehtap lived in New York with her second-generation American-of-Turkish-decent husband, Ahmed, who my grandparents had initially disliked.

Mehtap had won a scholarship many years before to an Ivy League university in the US, studying history, and that is where she met Ahmed, who was studying law.

For them, it was love at first sight, and for the four years that my aunt was at university, bar their lectures, they were rarely apart. When they both graduated, Mehtap, Ahmed and his family came to Northern Cyprus, so that Ahmed could ask for my grandfather's permission to marry his daughter.

When he asked my grandfather, he replied "No fucking way".

Mehtap requested to speak to my grandfather outside and after pleading with him for some forty-five minutes they came back in, and that was when my grandfather gave his blessing.

My aunt pretended to Ahmed's family that my grandfather had joking, but he was not.

The sight of my grandfather's shrouded body seemed too much for some to bear. As the terracotta coloured earth was thrown onto the stones, one of the aunts made a wailing type of noise.

As soon as we heard the sound, everyone turned around. Suddenly my mother and both sisters were on the ground. You could no longer see my mother, only her feet kicking in the air as she was fighting for her life under the combined 500 lbs weight of my two aunts.

We could hear my mother groaning, as both aunts had fainted and given their sheer mass, had taken my mother down with them. Relatives came rushing over to lift her sisters from on top of her.

Once my aunts came to, my mother politely moved to one side keeping a safe distance as she did not want a repeat of almost dying from suffocation.

Once the ceremony was over, we all began leaving the cemetery, Dilan came over with a smirk on his face.

"What are you smirking at Dilan?" I asked

"Just laughing about my mother and aunt Mehtap, given how big they are, I thought they would have been too big to fall without someone shouting timber."

I tried to hold back the laughter remembering where we were, but it was hard, as I kept on seeing the image of my mother's feet kicking in the air.

Chapter Nine

I'm Done

O nce the funeral had finished, everyone began making their way back to the house. While I was walking, I couldn't help but think about my grandmother and the single tear she had wiped away from her face during the funeral.

It had surprised me. My grandmother was burying the man she had spent most of her life with, the man with whom she had built a family with, a family that they, together, watched grow and expand.

It wasn't that she didn't care, as we all knew that my grandmother loved my grandfather, but she was just not one to ever show emotion. You would often hear her say how unrealistic some dramatic Turkish film was; often in a scene in which the main female character's love of her life had been murdered by the villain and was screaming in agony, realising that he had been ripped from her life.

To my grandmother it was unnecessary and over the top. She would often sit there watching, shaking her head the whole time with a scornful look on her face, disgusted by the extent of the emotion shown by the character.

It was stupid really. I have known my grandmother all of my life, and she has been pretty consistent. However, I don't know why suddenly I had expected her to have behaved uncharacteristically different at the sight of her dead husband. As though she would suddenly scream from the sheer distress of losing the man she had spent so many years with, throwing her herself into the ground where her beloved husband lay, but that wasn't who she was, and I think I may have seen too many Turkish films!

My grandmother's limited shows of emotion was something that the whole family would laugh about. Growing up my cousins and I would often mimic her, pretending to hug in an uncomfortable, robotic like way, laughing at how our grandmother hated all that touchy-feely stuff.

Though my mother was similar to my grandmother in so many ways, one thing where she was the counter opposite was when it came to showing emotion. Growing up in a house where her mother lacked any emotion and her father was strong and argumentative, it was almost as if, when she had her own family, she wanted to overcompensate for what she had lacked growing up. It was true that she often be brutal with her comments, but immediately after, she would then cuddle you or kiss you on the cheek. Everyone knew that she was a tactile person, especially when it came to her children.

We would always complain how she was embarrassing us, especially when our friends would come around to visit, she would just reply "I gave birth to you, you are always going to be part of me, so get over it."

Once I arrived back to the house, I found that my grandmother, my mother and three of my aunts were inside the bedroom where my grandfather's body had been, and they had closed the door behind them. They were in the room for a while, when my mother appeared in the kitchen.

As she walked into the kitchen, she didn't say a word, went straight to the back door and returned carrying a mop and bucket filled with steaming hot water and some banned detergent.

"Mum what are you doing?" I asked

"What does it look like? Cleaning the room, Mum wants to do it before the guests arrive", with that she quickly went back into the bedroom and closed the door again.

As she left the room, I saw two of my uncles look over at each other, both with a sly smirk on their faces. I immediately knew why they were laughing, but in defence of my mother, I looked straight at them, showing them I knew what they were doing.

They were laughing because it was known in my family that my mother was extreme when it came to cleaning.

Being the eldest daughter in such a large family, my mother, from a very young age, would assist her mother with cooking and cleaning. As she grew into an adult, cleaning became more of an obsession than a chore, and no matter how busy or tired she was, cleaning was part of her daily routine.

Friends and family would find the situation hilarious. A well-educated, successful specialist consultant in the US, who would often be found scrubbing toilets and wiping down surfaces.

Over the years, my parents had hired countless cleaners to help clean the house, given the gruelling hours they both worked. However they never actually lasted very long, as my mother would end up firing them, as they didn't meet her exacting standards.

My father would often argue with her, as the day before the cleaner came my mother would go around cleaning all of the kitchen and bathrooms. Whenever they argued, my mother's response was always the same "I am not going to have them think that we are dirty".

When the recently employed cleaner had finished cleaning, my mother would inevitably go around cleaning again as they had missed bits or not pulled everything out of the cupboards, as my mother had apparently expected.

She did, however, find one cleaner that lasted for over eight years, Rosa. My mother was devastated when Rosa had to stop working due to ill heath, partly given that she had grown really close to Rosa and also, given that she was naturally concerned about her. There was also a small part of her that also knew, that she would never find someone like Rosa again.

The kitchen and the two living rooms were full of people, all family and close friends. There were so many people in the house that there was barely any room to move.

I looked over and saw my aunt Lale sitting on the minder in the kitchen. I walked over to greet her, and she immediately jumped up and wrapped her arms around me.

"Are you, okay aunty?" I asked, by now her grip on me was tight, the whole time not saying a single word.

I was aware that aunt Lale had arrived in Cyprus a few days before, however, with everything going on, this was the first time I had seen her, other than at the funeral when she nearly suffocated my mother.

Aunt Lale, like most of the family, owned a holiday home in Cyprus and knowing how many people were coming to Cyprus for the funeral, decided to stay in her own home.

Though my grandparents had two properties, both were relatively modest three-four bedrooms, not large enough for all the family to stay in at the same time.

After a while, I could feel her tears rolling down my arm. "Aziz it is so nice to see you, I have missed you so much" she sniffed.

I was really close to my aunt growing up. When I decided to move over to London, it was one of the hardest decisions I ever had to make, as I left behind so many people that I cared about. I was aware that it wasn't just hard for me, but at the time, I was just so desperate for a fresh start.

"I know aunt, I miss you too. I will be coming back to Los Angeles to visit soon though". Even those words did little to console my aunt, and her grip was as tight as ever.

✷

When I told my family about my decision to move to the UK, everyone tried to talk me out it. I think at first, no one believed I would do it, however as I started making plans through my company who had offices in London, they all started realising that it actually was going to happen.

Once I had secured my new position, I moved over so quickly, that I had to initially stay with my aunt Ayse and her family. After four weeks of living with my aunt, I couldn't bear the constant arguments anymore nor my cousin Mehmet's constant smoking of marijuana, which left a distinctive smell and smog within the air, that I soon found an apartment to rent that was about forty minutes away from work.

Though I loved living and working in London, I did miss my family back in the US. It all happened so quickly that I never really got time nor gave enough time to my family regarding my decision to leave.

After a while, my aunt lightened her grip and kissed me on both cheeks, her face so puffy and wet from all the crying.

"Did you hurt yourself when you fell?" I asked. She immediately looked down to her leg, you could see the bruise already forming from where she fell on my mother during the funeral.

"Just a little, but I will be fine".

The door of the bedroom opened, and my grandmother came out. Two of my uncles went in and moved the table that my grandfather had been cleaned on. They immediately took the table to the back of the house.

At the front door, more and more guests were arriving; it is common for relatives and friends to offer their condolences to the family and bring a food offering.

I noticed that one of my grandmother's close friends had arrived. In all the years that I had known her, I realised that I never actually knew her real name, only the name that I had given her when I was a child.

Gilli Gulu, was a sweet old lady who lived in the village. She had originally come from a village up in the mountains near Kyrenia, however, had to move after the 1974 war. Sadly, during the war, her village was stormed, and all of her friends and family were killed. She had been on the outskirts of the village and upon seeing the soldiers, hid in a large clay oven. It took the soldiers two days to find her and when they did, they allegedly decided to cut out her tongue, so that she would not be able to tell people what she had seen.

Her nickname was born out of the sound and actions she would make. The first time I had met her, I was about 10 years old, and I had flown over with my family to visit our grandparents.

We were staying in the village house, and my mother and grandmother were taking coffee at her sister's house in the village.

I had gone to the café with my grandfather, and after getting bored, I decided to find my mother to annoy her.

When I arrived at the house, this sweet old lady got all excited, rushed over and kissed me on both cheeks.

Without her tongue, she was never again able to speak and was never taught how to use sign language. Instead, she made up her own gestures that everyone understood, and it was incredible to watch her and her friends have long conversations with her not using a spoken word.

When she would use her own sign language, she would make sounds that sound like Gilli and Gulu, which is the main reason why I gave her the nickname.

The first time I met her, I actually thought she was insulting me. Her gesture for a visitor from overseas was by touching her forehead and flapping her hand. I later learnt this was to indicate that I had flown there, which made sense after, but at the time it looked as though she was calling me a dick head.

Gilli Gulu had arrived with a big metal tray full of homemade Dolma, a dish consisting of rice and meat wrapped in vine leaves.

As she entered, she was kissing all of the family members she could see. The same large metal tray brought back a memory from another trip.

★

My cousins and I had stayed late at the village café, it was getting really dark as we walked through the village making it hard to see, you would only get some visibility as you got closer to the houses with lights on.

My cousins had decided that they would kick a can that they had found in the street like it was football and in all of the running around, they were slightly ahead of me.

Suddenly out of the darkness, a large metal tray came at me, hitting me straight in the stomach, the surprise and shock, made me scream out. On hearing my screams, my cousins came running back to investigate.

It turned out that Gilli Gulu had heard us coming close to her house. Earlier that day she had made some kofte that she wanted to offer to us. Given that she was unable to call out to us, she instead decided to get my attention another way.

We enjoyed eating the kofte, thanked her and continued back to the house. I spent the rest of the journey having to endure my cousin's laughter at how loudly I had screamed.

After Gilli Gulu, and countless other people arrived, each bringing plates of food or deserts. No one was eating, although the younger children running around the house took the opportunity to grab anything sweet, only to be told off later by their parents.

"Aziz, you need to go to the airport, your father and sister are arriving soon," my mother said.

My uncle Ilhan reluctantly gave me the keys to the Volvo, and as I was about to drive off, my cousin Dilan came running out of the house calling "Cuz wait for me".

As I drove down the main road from the village, my grandparents' house became smaller and smaller in the mirror, Dilan decided to begin playing with the radio in the car.

Turkish music was very distinct. Old-school music, much like the old crooners such as Frank Sinatra and Dean Martin, was considered modern arabesque or folk.

It would always feature the distinctive sound of the guitar like Saz and the vocals within the song would dominate. The words either made no sense like the famous song 'blue, blue more blue' or would be depressing, about how someone had broken the singer's heart, or that someone had died.

Though I like some of this sort of music, my cousin found a pop channel, which was playing one of the popular songs of the time and turned up the radio loud. The formula for a Turkish pop song is always the same, a good beat and for the singer to repeat the same words over and over again.

"Dilan, turn it down, we are meant to be in mourning," I said, as Dilan rolled his eyes and turned the radio down.

"You really need to chill out a little, cuz, you're too young to be this uptight". Dilan's words immediately struck a chord. My fiancé would often tell me that I was way too serious all the time and that I should act my age, but the problem, as the eldest child in the family, you are taught to act as a role model for your younger siblings.

I would have loved to be more carefree, but it was too ingrained in me now. "Yeah, and you need to learn to show some respect and grow up" I responded. There was a silence in the car for a brief moment.

"Did you see uncle Ilhan? I think he was crying", Dilan said with a big smile on his face. I wanted to say that it shouldn't matter if he cried, however, given our previous conversation, I decided to play along.

"No way! Mr big macho man crying" and we both started laughing.

I suddenly had to slam on the breaks hard, as a farmer in one of the neighbouring villages had decided to walk his animals onto the road, blocking the street.

"Move your bloody animals" Dilan shouted out the window of the car. The farmer just glanced over but ignored the remark.

The majority of the farmer's animals were goats with little bells on; it sounded more like a noise familiar to the Swiss Alps, not a village in Northern Cyprus. Though the road had been surfaced years before, on either side there was a range of plant life for the animals to feast on.

"He is fucking doing it on purpose," Dilan said as he jumped out of the car. I swiftly followed, but I was too late, Dilan had already threatened the farmer, and both were now arguing.

I dragged Dilan back to the car and then explained to the farmer that I was going to the airport to collect family. He eventually created a path to let us through, and as we drove past the farmer, he stuck two fingers up at Dilan. Dilan was not amused and kept on telling me to stop the car.

"I am so going to get him". Unfortunately for Dilan, he had inherited our grandfather's temper and was always getting himself into trouble.

By the time we arrived at the airport, Dilan had finally calmed down and was beginning to joke around again. The whole time we were waiting for my father and sister to come through the arrivals door, Dilan spoke most of his time and began pointing people out.

"Oh my god, look at the state of that" as Dilan pointed to a fat man in arrivals, whose t-shirt was only covering half of his stomach; "look at her, she thinks she is going to a wedding."

"Oh my god cuz, look at that man with the big teeth, did his mother have relations with a donkey?"

Luckily it was only a short wait until the automatic doors opened and I saw my father and sister walking towards us. As he came close, my father joked "Oh look Sila our chauffeurs have arrived".

"Aziz and Dilan here are our bags". It was clear that he was just kidding, but Dilan failed to see the humour and quietly under his breath, so my father could not hear said, "I'm done with this already".

As I had heard Dilan, I told him to stop, and immediately went over to greet my father and sister.

Chapter Ten

Pay My Own Way

✮ ✮ ✮

On the drive to Kyrenia, my father would not stop talking. Considering that both he and my sister had been travelling for over 17 hours, he was full of energy.

"Aziz, how is life in London?" he asked. Although my parents had come over to visit, my father still did not understand why I couldn't have stayed stateside and why I had to move so far away.

I always had the impression that they were waiting for me to say that I had made a mistake, and that I was coming home.

"Good thanks, Dad, I was promoted at work, and lately I have been getting some really good stories to work on."

Though my father was supportive of his children, I don't think my response was what he wanted to hear, so he turned his attention to my sister, who was already in a deep sleep.

"Wake up Sila, you need to stay awake to get used to the time difference". My father was a pragmatic man, my sister, on the other hand, was more like my mother, an iron clad will and unless she wanted to do something, you would have no chance of ever seeing it get done.

Sila briefly opened her eyes, looked at my father, made a noise and went back to sleep.

"How is Asim, uncle?" Dilan said it with a smirk on his face, it was like he saying a rude word from the way he was acting. My younger brother Asim was the oddball of the family. In their late teenage years, Dilan and Asim had become close as they realised they were kindred spirits, of a sort.

"Good thanks, Dilan, unfortunately, Asim had to stay behind because of his studies," my father said, which of course, we all knew was a lie.

In situations, such as this, my mother and father would agree on a strategy, a story that would be plausible so as not to raise suspicion, but that would also ensure that the family's reputation remained intact.

My family would rehearse these cover stories so much, that they would repeat it to anyone that cared to listen, forgetting on occasion, that they were speaking to someone that knew better.

My younger brother was not at all family orientated and had no interest in his parent's culture or his extended family. He tolerated my aunt Lale's family because it provided him with two accomplices to get up to mischief with.

He was the traditional bad boy at school, the one that would always get in trouble to get a laugh, and as a result had to repeat a few of years of school.

University took him to another level of trouble, joining a fraternity meant he had a brotherhood that he could regularly convince to join him in his fiendish plans. My parents would often get messages from the university regarding my brother's conduct.

I knew my parents were embarrassed, but no matter what they did, nothing ever seemed to stop Asim. If they cut him off financially, he would go to other members of the family asking for money, causing further embarrassment to my parents.

If they told him not to return home until he behaved, he would just stay at friends' houses, partying all the time.

Eventually, they came to the conclusion that they would only ever be able to limit the damage he could do and shame he could bring, but never stop or control him completely

Though Asim was academically average, he made up for it in sports. He was a natural sportsman and no matter what sport he tried, he picked it up quickly and was annoyingly good at it.

He went to university on a sports scholarship and played for his school's football team. To my father's annoyance, he would spend more time drinking and sleeping around with girls, than studying and you would often hear them arguing whenever they spent more than thirty minutes in the same room as each other.

You would often hear "You are wasting your life Asim, why aren't you more like your brother and sister".

My brother and I were never close, and when I told him that I was moving to London, he just laughed and said that I should grow a pair and move on.

"There are plenty more fish in the sea Aziz, you just need to stop trying to pick just one."

The only time I would ever receive any sort of communication from him, was often when he had exhausted our parent's patience, to the point where they refused to pay for something for him.

Then he would be the loving brother, with the sell at the end, "I hate to ask, but…"

As soon as my father blurted out the cover story, Dilan began to smile; given that he was close with Asim, he knew the truth and that my parents were covering for him.

"That is strange uncle, I got a message from him telling me that he was going to Disneyland with friends," Dilan said, clearly trying to agitate my father.

"He had better not be, he has to pass his exams this year, we are not paying for another year for him to mess around", my father's tone went from light hearted to angry.

"I don't know why it surprises you Dad, you know what Asim is like," I said.

Though Dilan enjoyed winding people up, he was always cautious with my father. Although he was pretty easy going, we all knew that he was like a sleeping elephant, and when provoked, could charge in and knock down walls. Fortunately for us growing up, his threshold was extremely high, so we rarely ever saw him angry.

"My mistake uncle," said Dilan realising that my father would not find his son's lack of respect amusing. We all knew that Asim would be going to Disneyland, regardless of what my father said.

Dilan's relationship with his father, on the other hand, was not a good one. Growing up as the eldest child, he was often made an example of and punished in front of the younger siblings as a form of warning to them all. There was though, a big contrast between the way his parents treated him, as his mother Lale, clearly favoured Dilan, and would often spoil him with gifts, even against her husband's wishes.

On one occasion Emir stole his father's car and drove it around the block. On the drive back, as he got closer to the house, he could not miss the sight of his angry father standing in the driveway. Emir got a slight beating for his crime, but Dilan's punishment was far worse. The punishment was unfair, as Dilan wasn't involved in the theft and at the time, and was in the neighbourhood on his bike, playing with friends. However, when he got home, his father was waiting to give him a beating. He told him that he should have been looking out for his younger brother and should stop him from doing these sort of things.

Uncle Hussein stopped beating Dilan the day he stopped crying. No matter what he used on Dilan or how hard he hit him, my cousin made no sound. The defiant look in Dilan's eyes must have unnerved my uncle, and although he would shout and argue with Dilan, he never used physical violence again.

Though Dilan would taunt and tease my parents, he loved them like his own parents they were like Yin, to his parents Yang. My parents were a safe haven for him and were incredibly supportive of my younger cousin.

"So uncle, how long are you here for" Dilan was clearly changing the subject.

"Only one week, it was hard to take time off work at the moment, but I had to be here for the family."

My father was extremely family orientated and my parents, though married for too many years to count were still very much in love, and my father adored my mother.

We would often catch him watching her adoringly. Of course, as children we would make sounds of disgust, but as adults, they became role models for the relationships we sought to have.

We had returned to the Kyrenia house, as this was where Nene wanted to spend the rest of her mourning period. With my grandfather's passing, my grandmother was now in a four month period of mourning, in which she would not able to go out. Should anyone go out during the mourning period, they would be the laughing stock of the community and people would see it as a lack of respect for their deceased relative.

As we pulled up to the house, it was hard to miss uncle Ilhan standing outside with a cigarette in his hand

"Welcome uncle," he said as he greeted my father.

"How are you Ilhan?", Ilhan just gestured with his face and shrugged his shoulders.

My father realising that Ilhan wasn't going to be very talkative, made his way to the house. Though we had just driven back to my grandparents' house, I suddenly realised that all four of the rooms were taken.

"Do you know where Sila will be staying?" as soon as the words had left my mouth, my mother came running out to greet my father. After they had held each other for a while, my mother turned to me and said

"Ayse has gone to stay with Mehtap, so Sila is staying here", my mother must have heard my question as she ran to my father.

"What do you look like Sila?" my mother said as Sila got out of the car. It was true, Sila looked a mess, she had an imprint of the car window seal etched into her face and was still not using words, merely grunting responses.

The house in Kyrenia was tranquil despite being quite full. As we walked into the kitchen, we could see my grandmother sitting writing at the table with my aunts and uncles surrounding her, just staring at her.

From a distance is looked like she was writing some meaningful words or thoughts regarding her husband, however as I got closer, I quickly realised that she was making a shopping list for things she needed my uncle to go and get.

"Are you okay Nene?" I asked as I kissed her on the cheek.

"Yes Aziz, glad it is over," she said.

"It was nice, so many people came to give their respects Nene" I responded.

"Hmm, they probably want to make sure he was actually dead! One of his so-called friends, had the cheek to come up and say that your grandfather was a good man and that he would miss him. The thing is Aziz, they hadn't spoken for thirty years!" I could see my aunts and uncles smiling.

Though everyone was in mourning, people knew what my grandfather was like, as he was known for arguing and annoying people, but he was still respected and liked.

As soon as my father walked into the kitchen, he went straight over to his mother-in-law. "I am so sorry we could not have been here sooner," he said.

"I appreciate you coming", with that they immediately hugged and kissed each other on the cheek.

My grandparents had a strange relationship with my father; they loved him but if anything went wrong with anyone in the family it was his fault. My grandmother would often say that I was like my mother and Asim was more like my father, putting the blame for my younger brother firmly on my father.

My father was very respectful and would just smile after any sarcastic comments from the family.

★

As the night wore on, one by one, family members left the house, leaving only those family members that were staying. It had been a very long day, and everyone agreed that we should all try to get some sleep.

After laying in bed for an hour or so, I was struggling to sleep, it was such a hot night, and the fan had minimal impact; it was so hot, that it felt like I had been breathing in pure fire.

To my cousins' annoyance, I refused to open the windows because I did not want to let in the array of bugs and mosquitos waiting to come in and attack me.

No matter what room, or what bed I slept in, you could pretty much guarantee that whoever I shared a room with, would be left alone and I would be the one under attack.

As I lay there, the heat was getting too much, so I decided to give into the bugs and mosquitos, and go up onto the roof.

The roof of my grandparents' house was flat and perfect for sleeping outside, and though you would have to wake up before the sun came up to avoid getting sun burnt, the breeze and clear skies were perfect for getting a good night's sleep.

Sleeping on the roof of houses was common in Cyprus, and if you drove late at night, you would often see people asleep facing the stars.

I opened the window and left the room leaving my two cousins in a deep sleep, apparently not as affected by the heat as I was.

As I went outside the house, I could see the ladder leading up to the roof. Each time I went up a rung of the ladder, I got slightly more nervous. The ladder didn't feel stable and well-constructed, and then I remembered why.

My grandfather would often go to buy goods, and when he saw the price would say "That is an insult, I could build that for half for price".

On returning home, he would set to work replicating what he wanted. The problem was that my grandfather was a government official and not a builder nor a carpenter.

Though his workmanship looked reasonable, when you looked closely or used the object, it would quickly become apparent that it wasn't well constructed.

I was too far up the ladder to stop, so decided to continue my climb, the higher I went, the more the ladder swayed in the breeze. I ran up the final four steps, for fear of it collapsing.

Once upon the roof, I found the perfect spot and put my bedding down on the ground. As I looked up to the sky, the stars and moon were so clear, clearer than I had ever seen them. It was like a painting where the artist had overemphasised the colour and shade of the moon and stars, by using much more brighter, vibrant colours. It was peaceful, so peaceful that I quickly fell to sleep.

About two hours later, I suddenly woke up, I could feel my nose running, I quickly realised that it was actually blood. As I stumbled to my feet, I looked over and saw that my two cousins had joined me and were already fast asleep.

They must have woken up in the night, realised I had gone and followed me to the roof. Maybe they were affected by the heat after all.

On the way down, I did not even think of the rickety old ladder and just came down as quickly as I could, as my priority was to stop the blood. Just before I entered the house, I heard a loud crunching and realised that I had just stepped barefoot on a cockroach.

With the blood still running down from my nose, I quickly scraped the cockroach from under my foot, and I entered through the back door into the kitchen.

Though I was in a rush to the bathroom, I did however notice that my grandmother was fast asleep on the minder in the kitchen. On discovering her although in a slight panic, I didn't want to wake her so I tried to tread as quietly as I could.

Once in the bathroom, I began washing my face tilting my head back, using tissue in each nostril. After a short while the blood had finally stopped, I started cleaning myself.

Walking back to the kitchen, I noticed there were blood stains all over the floor in the hall, leaving a trail back into the kitchen.

I quietly went back into the kitchen to get a cloth and retraced my steps, mopping up all of the blood I could find, being as quiet as I could.

The nose bleed did not deter me, and I decided that I would go back up onto to the roof as it was definitely cooler than the room. After braving the ladder again, I made my way over to my bedding on the ground. As soon as I was back in bed, a voice came out of the dark

"What happened? Are you okay?" I could tell by the voice it was Dilan.

"Just a nosebleed, nothing too serious," I said trying to play down the streams of blood that had just come out of my nose.

"God, you are such a baby, why does it always happen to you" he muttered before turning to go back to sleep.

Although what Dilan had said was true, I got irritated. Even though I was of Turkish Cypriot heritage with light olive coloured skin, I was the only one in my entire family that would regularly get sunburnt and prickly heat if I went out in the sun for more than thirty minutes at any time. I would always get bitten by mosquitos, while everyone around me was left intact and I suffered from nose bleeds when it was too hot.

In my anger, I looked at Dilan's back and said out loud "Yes, but at least I can fucking pay my own way in life".

As soon as I said it, I immediately regretted it. I knew he had heard, but made no sound.

Chapter Eleven

Stop Being A Baby

✮ ✮ ✮

In the morning, I felt even worse about what I had said to Dilan. Our circumstances had been very different growing up; where I had excelled at my studies, he was much more street smart, which served us both well in high school.

As children, we were inseparable and more like brothers than cousins. This was partly because we always lived nearby to each other and we both went to the same kindergarten, middle and high schools.

Not only did we see each other at school, but we also spent most weekends together. Like my parents with Dilan, Dilan's parents treated me like a son and whatever they were doing, I was included.

When we were younger, though different in many ways, Dilan and I also had a lot of common interests. This was especially true when it came to being a minority at a time when we were trying to fit in with wider society.

Though it was something that was always there, it only really noticeable, when we went to high school.

As we hit our teenage years, my interest and aptitude in my studies grew, whereas Dilan, struggled with learning and opted to become more of the class clown and rebel.

When people talk about segregation in society, it is clear that it starts in early development. Diversity in school is important, but groups do typically form, between those that identify with one another.

The mostly white, latino or black groups are a common sight in many high schools in diverse areas. It is likely that people find comfort being around people from the same ethnicity and social backgrounds as themselves and with people who 'get' them and their family situation.

The issue when you are a minority, is around identifying which group you best belong to. Being Turkish, you are too dark to be considered white, too light to be black and too muslim to be latino. That said, the group most Turkish boys identify themselves with and the group they are most accepted by, are the black groups.

The only group that race does not matter, is if you are a geek. Within the band of geeks, race and religion does not matter; as they see themselves as being unique or extraordinary special, whereas others see them as socially awkward.

The only consolation, is that this group of 'geeks' typically go on to be leaders in industry or invent the latest technology, but at high school, it is a challenging time that must be endured.

Where Dilan quickly became popular in the black group in high school, I became a fully signed up member of the geek club, as I never actually hid the fact that I liked studying.

As an adult, and listening to other geek alumni, I realised that I had avoided a lot of the typical high school experiences of being bullied or humiliated, and knew that this was mainly due to Dilan's protection. I was left alone to geek out because I was Dilan's cousin. No one forgot that if you messed with me, you messed with him.

It wasn't all one-sided though; where I excelled at school and Dilan struggled, I would often spend time trying to help him improve his grades.

A major upside to being part of the geek club, was that is where I met Ayla. The first time we met, she had just walked into the school's newspaper looking to join.

As she entered the room, she immediately fell flat on her face. She had not realised that one of her shoelaces was undone, catching on her other shoe as she walked in.

The baggy t-shirt she was wearing lifted from the gravitational pull, exposing her training bra as she lay lifeless momentarily on the floor.

As a teenager, any embarrassing event is typically life or death, but what Ayla did next made me really notice her.

She was clearly embarrassed, but rather than run out of the room, she jumped up from the floor, pulled down her shirt and shouted out "Please let me join the team, as you can see, I throw all of myself into everything I do" and everyone immediately roared with laughter.

Ayla wasn't a conventional beauty, but her personality and outlook on life made her the most beautiful woman I had ever seen.

Ayla was Turkish-American like me, but her family were very different to mine. Where my academic ability was something that came naturally to me, for Ayla, though smart, she was always driven to do better. If she got an A for an assignment, next time she wanted an A+. Her drive was as a result of her family and upbringing.

Ayla was one of six children and the only girl. Where my parents were professional and were living the white collar American dream, Ayla's family were firmly blue collar.

Ayla's parents came over to the US in the early 1970s seeking a better life. Her father was a tailor in Turkey, and her mother was a seamstress. When they first arrived, they took a string of low-paid sewing jobs, eventually saving enough money to buy a dry cleaners.

Seeing her family struggle, drove Ayla, and she was determined to become a doctor. As we went through high school and later college, our love seemed to grow each year, and everyone knew I was in trouble, when I was 18 years old.

Ayla went to Turkey for a 3-month vacation with her family. On the lead up to her leaving, I kept on telling everyone that I was fine about it. However, when the day finally arrived, I was devastated and quickly fell apart.

I felt part of me was missing, and after seeing me crying in my room, my mother decided to get me an earlier flight to Cyprus to visit my grandparents. Though she didn't say it, I actually believe she had booked a much earlier flight so that she wouldn't have to see me moping around the house anymore.

The moment I arrived, I immediately began wearing down my grandfather to take me to Istanbul to visit Ayla. After three days of constant begging, my grandfather gave in and took me to Istanbul. To save face, he claimed he had business in Istanbul. However, it was evident he did it for me.

Though my parents were progressive in so many ways, sometimes the old-world traditions came through.

As the eldest son from a well-educated and respected family, I was considered marriage gold. In olden times, I would have been promised at birth to advance the family, so seeing me pining for Ayla seemed to un-nerve my parents as I don't think they had realised how serious we were, until the Istanbul vacation.

They both liked Ayla, but they made it clear to me one evening that I could do better. The conversation resulted in an argument, in which I told them that I was 18 years old and would go out with whomever I wanted. I went on to say that if they wanted us to be traditional, they should have stayed in Cyprus.

My parents were not happy, but part of what made me love them so much, was that the love for their family was more important to them over anything else, and they soon accepted my position and never discussed it again.

Throughout college, Ayla and I were still inseparable, and when I graduated, my parents surprised us by paying for us to go on a trip to Paris.

It was such a beautiful and romantic vacation that the mood took me, and I proposed. I had no plans to propose and clearly wasn't prepared. I didn't even have a ring, I just knew at that moment that, I wanted to marry her.

We were walking through the Luxembourg Park, it was a beautiful sunny day, and before I knew it, I was on the floor proposing.

Looking back, it wasn't the most romantic proposal. We were both hot, I went down on one knee next to the men's toilets, and I had no ring to give Ayla. However she accepted, and we both laughed about the proposal when we told friends and family back home.

When we got back to the states, our families both felt we were too young, but respected our decisions. My parents were happier when I told them that we planned to marry after Ayla had finished her medical studies.

★

The years went by really quickly, and soon after Ayla had become a doctor, preparations for our marriage immediately started. My mother and Ayla's mother took over, so neither of us had much say in our wedding, however, we were both thrilled just to be finally getting married.

The day of the wedding came round quickly, and I was excited that I was finally getting married. By now Ayla was a junior doctor at the local hospital and was working really long shifts. My career was also taking off, which meant I was out on assignment a lot.

We hadn't spent an enormous amount of time together leading up to the wedding due to our work commitments, but neither of us was worried as we knew that we would both soon be spending the rest of our lives together, or so I thought.

My parents had booked a 4-star hotel in downtown Los Angeles, the only one big enough to house hundreds of relatives that were going to be attending. A week before the wedding, the family had begun arriving from all over the world, and my parent's home quickly became extremely stressful.

My mother, not only had to deal with the upcoming wedding preparations, but also the annoying habits of the relatives staying at our house.

The plan for the wedding day was to initially go to the registry office to get formally married in the eyes of the law and then to go to the hotel to have the more traditional Turkish ceremony.

We had over 700 guests attending, 500 from my side and 200 from Ayla's side of the family. In addition to my family, my parents, brother and sister had been inviting their friends, and I had asked my friends from high school, college and close colleagues from work.

Knowing Ayla's family circumstances, my parents offered to pay for the majority of the wedding. Ayla's father was initially a little offended, but I guess the thought of how expensive this was likely to be, he soon thanked my parents.

That last week before the wedding was hell for Ayla and I. Not only did we have work pressures, we also had family members constantly teasing us, trying to shock us with marriage stories or providing us with unsolicited advice on the secret to a long marriage.

The advice would either be a veiled disgruntled joke such as" the secret to a good marriage is to drink every day" or a downtrodden remark like "never disagree with your wife or your mother".

I remembered the day of the wedding so well. I was exhausted as I had hardly slept the night before. However, I was so excited that it was like my body had too much adrenaline to care about the lack of sleep.

It was a beautiful sunny day, and the sunshine streamed into my room as I threw open my bedroom blinds. I could smell food coming up from downstairs and people talking outside my room, they were trying to whisper talk, however when speaking Turkish it appears it is hard to speak quietly.

As soon as I was up, I started to feel a sort of nervous excitement. I sat up in bed as my parents knocked and entered my room.

"We are so proud of you son, you have always known what you wanted," my mother said, crying as she spoke, tears rolling down her cheeks.

Though I knew why she was crying, it still upset me, and although those were happy tears, it was really rare to see my mother cry.

When I started to get ready, my mobile phone made its usual noise to tell me I had just received a text message. I immediately picked it up and saw it was a message from Ayla.

I began to open it, thinking it was some message telling me how excited she was. I read the message which said, "I love you so much, but I can't do this, I am so sorry." Ayla had a dark sense of humour, so I called her to laugh with her

"Ha ha ha Ayla, very funny," I said as she answered the phone

"I am so sorry" she replied. It was clear that she was crying and I immediately knew that either this was a really sick joke or it was no joke at all. As soon as she said she was sorry, she hung up.

I must have called her 100 times, but she never again answered the phone, and each time it went to straight to voicemail. I left her so many messages that her mailbox quickly became full, and then I just go an unavailable message, whenever I called.

That didn't stop me, and I kept on calling, hoping she would answer, laughing, telling me that it was all a big joke and that she couldn't wait to get married.

Looking back now, it was evident I was in shock. However, I don't remember all of the events that followed the call with Ayla. I remember wanting to go and drive to see Ayla, however before I could leave my room, my parents had come rushing in.

Ayla's father had called my father to tell him what was going on. My father later had said that Ayla's father was crying on the phone, he had been upset and he was calling to apologise, while at the same time wanting to respect his daughter's wishes.

When I told them I was going to see Ayla, my father asked me to sit down.

"Son," he said, "I am so sorry", with those words my father put his arms around me.

The moment he held me, I began to sob uncontrollably. While in his arms, I could feel his body shaking, as he was crying with me in his arms. My mother came over and held both of us in her arms, all of us crying.

✯

I didn't want to leave my room, and I couldn't face the world. My family tried to console me, but I actually felt such a great loss that I couldn't speak or even entertain the idea of talking to anyone. So each day, they would take it in turn to come in, sit down, speak to me, and after twenty to thirty minutes of me laying there motionless, they would leave.

Although some soon got bored, that never stopped my mother. She would frequently come throughout the day to bring me food and would sit there stroking my hair. She kept on telling me that everything will be okay and would often leave taking the previous trips food away with her.

I was sad about Ayla, but I was also embarrassed. Was there something wrong with me? Why would she leave me on the day of our wedding like this? Was there someone else? I had so many thoughts going through my head.

My phone would often buzz from a new text message, but I would only check to see if it was from Ayla, once I realised that it wasn't and was a text message from a friend or colleague, I would just leave it unread.

I knew I was numb to life, trying to work through my grief and trying to think about what I was going to do next, I only had a plan A, which was to marry Ayla and start a family with her. There had never been a plan B.

I just kept on wondering what I could have done differently, and why she was doing this to me, but the answers never came.

I remember thinking once about taking my own life. I had never thought of it before, but the shame, and feelings of rejection made me feel like I couldn't go on. However, as soon as the thought crossed my mind, I began thinking of my family, my parents, my brother and sister, and no matter how bad I felt, I couldn't do that to them.

After about two weeks, Dilan came to visit. I thought it was the first time, however I later found out that he had been three or four times. He walked into my room looking angry.

"Az stop being a baby, she was a bitch for what she did to you, but you need to man up," he said as he sat down on my bed.

"Fuck off Dilan" I replied

"What, like the way me and all of your friends fucked Ayla, cuz, I have to tell you, she wasn't even that good a shag" Dilan replied with a smirk on his face. Clearly, he was joking, but Dilan mocking Ayla had actually weirdly helped.

We spoke for about half an hour, and eventually, he talked me into going downstairs, which was the first time I had left my room in weeks. I don't recall if I had ever thanked Dilan for what he did.

Chapter Twelve

We Will See About That

The next morning, I was awoken by a burning sensation on my head, arms and legs, I had clearly not woken up before the sun, and by now the heat and sun rays were close to full strength.

I looked over and saw that my two cousins were both still sleeping, however clearly less affected by the sun than I was. Both had thrown the covers off, and their backs and legs were glowing, as the sun shone down on their skin.

After a number of attempts to wake them, including kicking them a few times, they reluctantly got and up made their way to the ladder.

Dilan was the first to go down the ladder, which he did with such ease; he was fearless. Next, it was my turn, though I had managed to go up, and quickly back down when my nose began to bleed, in the bright sunshine, when I could see all the dangers, it wasn't so easy.

As soon as I was on the second rung of the ladder, I could feel my legs seizing up, as the unstable structure of the ladder swayed. I was trying to remain positive, and repeatedly told myself I could do it. However, I was getting more and more nervous, and my legs were visibly shaking.

It was strange, as in the past I had never suffered from vertigo, but this was different, it wasn't a fear of heights, and it was more a fear of being on an unsafe structure made by my grandfather in an attempt to save money.

"Hurry up and come down you stupid idiot," Dilan said, as both he and his brother began to laugh.

"Don't let go of the bloody ladder you fool, and stop laughing, it is not helping", as I shouted to my cousins, I quickly moved down another rung.

The laughter was coming from both above and below, and I was finding it hard to concentrate.

I took each rung at a time, and every time I managed a new rung, I would cling on for dear life for a brief period, before attempting the next rung.

After manoeuvring my way down slowly, when I got to a safe distance, I decided to jump off. Once I landed safely, I was so happy to be firmly on terra firma.

Leaving my two laughing hyena cousins behind, I walked into the kitchen to find the room full of relatives. My mother, father, sister and grandmother were all seated at the kitchen table and my uncle Ilhan, although having clearly just arrived at the house, was already beginning to grab the food on the table closer to him, including the solid brick like cheese.

"Big day today Aziz. Today you are going to become a man" uncle Ilhan said with a mouth full of food. As he said it, some of the food came flying out to my sister Sila's disgust.

Sila was looking at uncle Ilhan in shock at his bad manners, and she had the look of a person that was trying to stop herself from doing or saying something, willing herself to ignore it and let it pass.

"Do you want me to come with you Aziz?", my father asked, but before I could reply uncle Ilhan began taunting.

"Aww, do you want daddy to hold your hand for you, Aziz?"

Though everyone in the family was used to uncle Ilhan, my father was clearly not in the mood for him and gave him a look that said as much.

"It is okay Dad, you have just arrived and should rest" I responded. The truth is, I wanted nothing more than my father to come along with me, but it wouldn't have been fair to him.

★

After breakfast, uncle Ilhan and I made our way over to the Volvo, as we got close, uncle Ilhan in a so-called joking way said: "Want me to open the door for you, your highness?" I just ignored him and got into the car.

The journey to Nicosia was torture, my uncle had purposely taken us the villages route, just to see soldiers on the roads.

It was common in Cyprus, for a village in a prominent location to have an army base. As you drove near the base, you would typically see a large fence and two soldiers outside standing guard.

Every time we went past an army base, uncle Ilhan's remarks were along the lines of "Oh look that will be you soon", "I wonder if you will be stationed here" and "Do you want me to ask the General for a uniform that matches your eyes?"

The insults became wearing, and though I tried to ignore him, he made it hard.

After passing what must have been the fifth base, I started to wish that I had asked one of my other uncles or cousins to come along for the ride, at least I would have had temporary relief in between my uncle's remarks. However knowing them, they would have more than likely joined in.

When we arrived at Nicosia, the first port of call was the Police Headquarters, where I was required to register.

The police headquarters was a large building, and it was clear to see, what it was, given the number of police officers standing near to the entrance, and police vehicles parked at the front of the building. When we arrived in the building, we spoke to the stern looking receptionist, who sent us down a long corridor to a large room.

Once we were in the room, we spotted a couple of empty seats. The room was full of people. Although this was a police headquarters, none of the individuals in the room was there to report a crime but instead were there to register for government-related services.

There was only one police officer in the room, and he was close to the door, seated on a large stool behind a sort of lectern.

Every time anyone would arrive, he would ask for their name and the purpose of their visit.

After sitting down for a few minutes, the guy sitting next to uncle Ilhan informed us that we had to get a number, however by then a few more people had arrived, clearly pushing us to the back of the queue. It was a shame the police officer hadn't thought to tell us this when we arrived!

The room didn't have air conditioning but was cooled by big fans on full speed on the ceiling.

After only ten minutes uncle Ilhan began complaining loudly enough that everyone could hear "how long are we going to have to sit here, how fucking hard can this be."

Though I occasionally nodded to whatever my uncle was saying, I was more interested in the conversations going on around me and actually heard very little of what he was saying.

Sitting next to me was a woman, who was a French national that had just moved to Northern Cyprus, and was registering with the police. Next to her was a man from Germany, who sounded like was having to go through a similar process as I was.

The man from Germany looked as nervous as I did. However, he was fortunate as he didn't have any member of his family with him, taunting him and making the situation a lot worse than it should have been.

After about forty minutes, uncle Ilhan was getting even more frustrated, and in between a large huff, he said: "This is too fucking much."

A young nervous-looking police officer entered the room, spoke briefly to the officer stationed at the door, and walked over to us and asked that we follow him. As we left the room, we could hear the people left behind complaining that we had jumped the queue.

We were taken down a long corridor. Even though we asked where we were going, the young police officer ignored us and kept on walking.

The officer finally stopped outside a closed door, which had the words 'Police Commissioner' written on it.

He knocked three times and shortly after we heard a loud deep voice shout "Come in".

As we entered the office, the young as immediately dismissed, and a large, overweight, moustachioed man stood up.

"Welcome, I am sorry to have kept you waiting. Unfortunately, I told the officers to notify me, as soon as you arrived, but the news had only just come through".

Uncle Ilhan was quick to reply "Not at all, we have only just arrived". My uncle's sudden backtracking after his constant moaning surprised me, and I must have clearly had a visible look of shock on my face as uncle Ilhan went a little red in the face.

We quickly established that the police commissioner was an old friend of my grandfathers', and when he found out that I was coming, he told his staff that he was going to personally oversee my naturalisation.

The police commissioners name was Mohammed, and though he had an amiable, jovial manner about him, it was also apparent, that he probably wasn't always like this.

"Your grandfather Aziz, was a great man, he and I did national service together many years ago."

Mohammed went on to explain, that on one occasion he, and my grandfather were stationed outside an army base to keep watch, it was a sweltering day, and they were both really thirsty, and getting very dehydrated. To leave the post is punishable, but my grandfather couldn't bear it anymore.

They made a plan, and my grandfather made his move. He abandoned his post, and went to the neighbouring village to get drinks and supplies.

Fortunately for my grandfather, he managed to return undetected. Their insubordination was discovered when they mistakenly forgot to discreetly dispose of the empty bottles, and snacks wrappers.

My grandfather was beaten for abandoning his post, afterwards Mohammed spoke to my grandfather and apologised for not admitting that he drank and ate the snacks as well. My grandfather simply replied, "We drank, we ate, and we are alive, the bruises will go, so don't worry about it."

While Mohammed and my uncle continued reminiscing about my grandfather, I began looking around the room. Mohammed's office was huge with minimal furniture; just a large desk and a few chairs in the room.

Behind Mohammed's desk was the Turkish Cypriot flag and the traditional bust of Kemal Ataturk. The walls were painted in the official police coloured pale blue, and all across the walls were various certificates and awards.

The room was somewhat intimidating, and though our host was friendly and gracious, you could imagine how imposing the room could be under different circumstances.

★

Suddenly the police commissioner's tone changed "Right we must now go to the army to register."

As we left the police station, Mohammed insisted that we went with him in his car. We walked over to his huge 4 by 4 police vehicle and got in. Uncle Ilhan sat up front, and throughout the journey, both he and Mohammed continued telling stories about my grandfather.

It took us about twenty minutes to get the army base, and as we pulled up, it was evident to see that it was more an office, than the military base I was expecting.

When we had arrived at the police headquarters, I had no idea of the procedure or what was going to happen and just went with the flow. This was no different.

As we entered the military office, I immediately saw my great uncle Osman, the brother of my grandmother. I had seen uncle Osman at both the funeral and the house. However, I didn't actually get to speak to him, as there were swarms of people around him the whole time.

"Welcome nephews," he said as everyone greeted each other.

"Aziz, your grandmother called, and asked that I personally come and look after you."

There was a buzz in the office, as it seemed that it was rare for this modest office to receive such notable guests as the police commissioner and an army general.

Uncle Osman was a general in the Turkish Cypriot army, and was both heavily decorated, and well known within Northern Cyprus. Though he was now old, and retired, he still had a presence about him.

A soldier came over to commence the procedure, and asked that I follow him, uncle Osman joked that the soldier had better look after me or else. Unfortunately, the soldier didn't get the joke and immediately went bright red.

The soldier took me to a small adjourning room, and I was handed a laminated piece of paper, and told to practice reading it. The soldier left the room, leaving me to learn it on my own.

The piece of paper had the Turkish Military oath on it, and though it was something I had heard before, reading it made me a little nervous.

After being given a few minutes to practice, I was taken back out to where my uncles and Mohammed were standing. I was told to start reading aloud when I was ready. So as not to embarrass me, uncle Osman began saying the oath with me, and Mohammed joined in shortly after.

Though I didn't want to be naturalised, I decided to go with the flow, and read the oath out loud, although it was hard for me to be heard, as everyone else in the office had joined in at this stage.

Once the oath ceremony was completed, I was then handed some papers to read and sign. I did a quick read through, then completed all of the required information. The previously red-faced soldier than placed a stamp on the official looking document.

"You can visit Cyprus for no more than 90 days on any one occasion, if you stay for longer, you will be required to carry out national service" the soldier informed me.

Once everything was finished Mohammed invited us all, including uncle Osman, back to his office to take coffee. Uncle Ilhan went back with Mohammed, while I joined uncle Osman.

Uncle Osman led me to his old S Class Mercedes. As we got in, it was evident to see that the sun had cracked the leather seats, and age had worn the interior.

"It is so nice to finally speak to you Aziz, how have you been?"

"I have been good thank you uncle, after moving to London, my life has been very different, but it has been good for me."

Uncle Osman, though a serious man, had a kind face and it was easy to see that he and my grandmother were siblings.

"Your grandmother told me what happened to you Aziz, don't let people change who you are. When you meet the right person, everything will happen, as it was meant to be"

I knew uncle Osman was trying to be supportive, but it was hard talking about my former fiancé, I just nodded, and smiled, so as not to be rude.

"Aziz, I know your grandmother is a strong woman, losing your grandfather is hard for her, just give her time, and she will be herself again."

It was strange hearing uncle Osman say this. Since finding out about my grandfather, my grandmother had been no different, still the same grandmother that I had always known.

★

We pulled up at the police station, and made our way to Mohammed's office. Uncle Ilhan and Mohammed had already arrived, and even had enough time to get the coffees ordered.

Ever since meeting uncle Osman at the military office, uncle Ilhan was a different person. He wasn't joking around, he was attentive and kept asking me if I was okay and was trying to explain what was going on.

"Are you okay?" I asked him. It was as though body snatchers had taken him over.

As the Turkish coffees turned up, uncle Osman turned to me and asked: "So Aziz, do you feel different now that you are a Turkish Cypriot Citizen?"

"Yes uncle, I can feel the moustache growing already" I replied, everyone started laughing.

After all the taunting on the way up to the police station, I never actually spoke to uncle Ilhan about his experiences in the army.

"Where did you do your national service?" I asked, as all eyes darted to uncle Ilhan. I then went on to explain that my uncle had told me some army stories on the way up to Nicosia to reassure me. I was being sarcastic, but the two officials were unaware of my journey to the capital.

Uncle Ilhan started going really pale, and he mumbled quietly "I haven't done my national service" very word spoken, seemed painful for him.

"How did that happen?" uncle Osman said as he started to chuckle to himself "We will have to see about that."

Chapter Thirteen

Everyone Shits

After thanking the two men, we left the police headquarters, and began the drive back to Kyrenia. Unlike the journey to Nicosia, this time. Uncle Ilhan took the more direct route and hardly spoke, only initially asking if I wanted the air conditioning on.

"Sorry about the National Service uncle". When I had been told that I had to be naturalised, my grandmother had begun immediately trying to reassure me by telling me that it wasn't an issue, as none of her sons had done their national service.

"It is okay, and sorry for teasing you Aziz, I was just trying to make a joke of it, so as not to make it a big deal".

I immediately felt bad as uncle Ilhan, for the first time, was sincere. What had I become, in my desire to get a little revenge for all his taunting, I had not only stooped to a new low, but I had embarrassed my uncle in front of people he respected.

Once the apology had been said, uncle Ilhan began to speak more frequently. However, he was acting very different to the uncle I was used to, talking without his usual brand of both joking, and insulting, all at the same time.

"Life is way too short", uncle Ilhan said as he went on to explain that three years ago, he found a lump near his groin.

"I never knew," I said, shocked,

"No one in the family knew except for your mum and, well, you now," he replied.

He continued explaining that the lump kept on growing, and in the end, he had no choice but to seek medical attention. They cut out the piece and ran a biopsy, only to find out it was cancerous.

Uncle Ilhan was getting emotional as he told me that while he waited for the results, he was adamant he was going to die.

He had to eventually tell his wife because one night she found him in their youngest daughter's room. He was watching his daughter sleeping, crying quietly thinking about her growing up without her father.

Fortunately, the removal of the lump, and treatment he underwent, had isolated the growth, and he was now cancer-free.

"I am so sorry uncle, I never knew," I said still in shock.

"That is why it is important to enjoy life Aziz, life is so short, and you never know when it will end."

"Do you want a drink uncle?" I asked. At this point, I felt I owed him a drink after he had gone out of his way to take me to be naturalised. Especially after flagging up to the police and army that he had somehow avoided doing national service, and in light of these new revelations, I was now feeling even more guilty about everything.

"Why not," he said, with a smile. Though we were half way back to Kyrenia, uncle Ilhan decided that he wanted to drink in the café, in the village. Despite being on the highway, uncle Ilhan did a u-turn when he saw a gap in the traffic, almost forcing us to go into a ditch. It all happened so quickly that I didn't even get time to register what he had done until we were driving in the opposite direction.

★

Once we arrived at the village, we drove directly into the centre, and as we got closer to the café, I could see there were a lot of people already there.

We parked right outside the cafe, and immediately we could hear a group of old men in the café in fits of laughter. We both quickly walked over to find out what was going on.

The men were struggling to tell us the story, as each time one of them began to speak, it would set the others off in fits of laughter.

Eventually, we established that the story related to a man from the village, who was found alive after he had been missing for three days.

It transpired that on the day the man disappeared, he had been driving from Nicosia to Kyrenia. It was a hot day, and he had an old car.

Due to the heat, and the fact he had no air conditioning, the man had every window of the vehicle open. He began smoking a cigarette but hadn't factored the suction that was caused by the speed he was going on the highway.

The lit cigarette flew out of his hand, came straight back into the car through the open rear window.

The sight of smoke from the back of the car panicked the driver, and he began turning around, attempting to pat out the still lit cigarette.

Not looking at the road, he saw the huge ditch he was heading towards when it was too late for him to react.

The builders had dug out the ditch some time ago to enable some of the service companies to work on the pipes that ran underneath the highway. When the car went down the ditch, the man, fortunately, did not suffer any injuries, which in itself was a miracle given how fast he was going.

The problem for the man, was that the ditch was so deep that you could not see his vehicle from the highway without actually going alongside it and looking down. No one saw the man's accident, so no police or ambulance was called to his aid.

The incident occurred on a Friday resulting in the man not being discovered for three days until the builders returned to work on Monday.

For three days, the man was trapped in the vehicle with the harsh sun beating down. When he was discovered he was immediately taken to hospital, as he had severe dehydration. The old man telling the story, still laughing said: "This is typical of Mutlu, he is such an idiot".

The old man explained that when he was found, he had stripped off all of his clothes, was delirious through sunstroke, and had been found drinking his own urine.

After listening to the story, I decided it was about time I got a drink, and I felt it only polite to offer the men as well. After ordering 16 beers, 12 Turkish Coffees and 4 bottles of coke, I sat down.

"Thanks, Shit Boy," one of the men said, and everyone burst out into laughter again.

A nickname I had long forgotten, but I also seemed to have forgotten that no one forgets anything in Cyprus.

Cypriots have memories like elephants, and could easily recall events from twenty or more years ago, especially if it was an embarrassing one. However, they would often embellish the story to get more laughs.

On one of my trips in my youth, my cousins and I went to the café and were playing pool until late. Back then my body was even more sensitive than it is now, and any little thing would set it off.

I was getting overly confident that my body had somehow improved, and made the mistake of eating a fresh cucumber earlier in the evening.

About two hours later, my stomach began cramping, so I decided to go to the toilet. Though I had been to the café a number of times, I had never actually used the bathroom before.

When I walked in, I was shocked to see a hole in the ground. Literally a giant hole in the ground with a tap and bucket next to it.

The toilet had been used a fair bit, and the smell was unbearable. After seeing something move from within the hole, I decided it was a little too rural for me and left.

Toilets like this were not uncommon, but the vast majority of people had, like my grandparents, installed a plumbed in bathroom.

After telling my cousins that I would be back, I quickly left on my way back to the house to use the nicely plumbed in western toilet that I was used to.

My cousins had offered to come back with me, but I could tell that their offer was insincere, as they clearly wanted to continue playing pool, so I told them not to worry as I knew that I would be quick.

It was really dark away from the café, and in my haste, I missed the turnoff for the shortcut back to the house. By the time I realised I was already half way, and so continued with the long route home. It seemed that every house I passed had people on the veranda drinking, and eating in the very dim light. As it was a hot evening, everyone was sitting outside, probably in the hope that there would be a breeze to cool them down.

On seeing me, they would often call out to greet me, but I couldn't stand still for too long, and would just reply briefly, and kept on moving. I didn't want to appear rude to people. However, my stomach by now was cramping more frequently, which was becoming extremely painful.

I was finally getting closer to the house, but before I could get there, I had to pass the house of a girl that, at the time, I was besotted with. This girl was so beautiful; she had long straight black hair, her skin was unblemished and her features so perfect, it was like they had been crafted.

If she was anywhere else, she could have easily been on the catwalk at any fashion show, and given her looks, there was already a long list of suitors' queueing up for her, including me.

As I walked past her house, a number of her family were outside drinking Ayran, a traditional drink, made of yoghurt, water and dried mint.

"Aziz, welcome, how is your family?" her mother called out.

"Fine thanks, aunt, how are you all?" I paused, however as soon as the words came out, my body was no longer my own, and without warning, the entire contents of my stomach, including the cucumber, were now in my underwear, and began seeping through my shorts.

In the fear that she would come over, close enough to see what I had just done, I told her that my grandparents, and cousins would come by to visit in a few days, and that my grandmother was waiting.

"Please do, it would be great to see you all," she said as I quickly departed.

I tried running away, but it was difficult, with what felt like a backpack stuffed in my pants. Even with diarrhoea dripping down my legs, I was just more relieved that she didn't see what I had done, which might have ruined any chance I might have had with her daughter.

As I struggled back to the house, I only saw one old man on a donkey, however, so as to avoid any embarrassment I moved into the ditch alongside the road to avoid detection.

Once at the house, I rushed inside, it was dark as my grandmother had clearly gone to bed, so I went straight into the bathroom.

I immediately sat on the toilet, but there wasn't much point as the entire contents of my stomach were already all over me.

I got up, emptied what I could from my underwear into the toilet, and left my clothes to soak in the sink. I jumped into the shower, however with no sunlight and countless people having showers throughout the day, the water by now was freezing.

Though it was cold, this time I didn't care, I just wanted to be clean. As I went into the bedroom, I remember thinking that I had got away with it, without anyone knowing, I rinsed off my clothes and placed them into the washing machine, and retraced my steps to mop up any spillage that had occurred on the floor.

As soon as I finished putting the cloth in the sink, the door to the kitchen burst open, it was Dilan.

"Cuz you have been ages, are you coming back?" his voice was a mixture of concern and frustration at having to leave the café.

I was close to Dilan and trusted him, so I told him what had happened. He roared with laughter, so loud that he woke my grandmother up.

She came into the kitchen to find out what was going on. When I began to tell her what had happened, Dilan kept on adding more dramatic elements to my story, such as "the old man smelt the shit, and blamed the donkey".

My grandmother could not control her laughter, so much that a little pee came out, causing her to rush to the bathroom.

Upon her return, we all agreed not to tell my grandfather or my other cousins, for fear that it would be spread around the village.

The next morning, I went with my cousins to the café, only to have this elderly man shout out on my arrival "Feeling better now shit boy, want some cucumber?" and with that everyone in the café began laughing.

I quickly established that my grandfather had found my rinsed clothes in the washing machine. After asking why they were in there, my grandmother tried to create a cover story, but he could tell she was lying, and after some interrogation, he eventually got the truth out of her.

He promised her that he wouldn't tell anyone, but the temptation of a good story was too great, and he likely told everyone the moment he arrived at the café, and so that is how the nickname 'shit boy' started.

"You never told me about this, shit boy", uncle Ilhan said, with tears in his eyes from laughing so much. Looking at him, I couldn't help feel that his change of personality was short lived and the old uncle I knew only too well, was returning.

At this point, I decided to get up and sit somewhere else before uncle Ilhan ruined our bonding time.

I walked over and sat down next to a man I had spoken to a number of occasions before. The man's name was Oscan, and he was a teacher from the local school. He was a really nice guy, and seemed pleased when I came over.

Many years ago, when I first met Oscan, we began talking, and suddenly I heard my grandfather's voice shout across "Aziz, don't talk to that idiot".

I never found out why they did not like each other. However, he had always nice to me, and we always had good conversations. After my grandfather had shouted at me, and when I had finished the talking with Oscan, I walked over close to where my grandfather was seated, and as I got closer, I heard him tell the group loudly enough for me to have heard, that "families should stick together".

What my grandfather wasn't aware, was that my mother had previously told me, that if I observed every one of my grandfather's vendettas, I would never talk to anyone, and had been told just to be polite, and not to ignore anyone.

As I finished catching up with Oscan, the café owner, Mustafa came over.

"Welcome Aziz, sorry we haven't had a chance to speak yet" with that he handed me a drink.

I had always liked Mustafa, he was a quiet type but was one of those people that had a love-hate relationship with my grandfather.

One reason for this up, and down relationship, was due to us grandchildren. On one of our many visits to Cyprus, my cousins and I stayed at the café, late one evening.

The inner part of the café was made of two parts. The first was where the drinks were served and was also where the TV was situated, and along with a number of tables for customers who wanted somewhere to sit, that was a bit cooler than the outside shaded veranda.

The second part, connected via a door, was the games room. It had three pool tables, two dart boards and six video game machines. The games room was the place that my cousins, and I spent most of our evenings in Cyprus.

On one particular evening, we were told by Mustafa that he was closing, and that it was time to go. As we were getting our stuff, we could see most of the old men going into the TV room, rather than going home.

We left as instructed, and circled back. We were careful not to be seen, and as we arrived back at the café, we were shocked. Mustafa had put a Turkish pornographic movie on the television. They are usually funny to watch as the woman is extremely loud, you don't see that much, and the whole time she is bobbing up and down, still firmly wearing her headscarf.

The old men were gathered round all with their hands in their pants, as they watched the movie. We eventually left, laughing at the old perverts.

Still laughing when we got home, our grandfather asked what was so funny. When we told him the story, he was not amused. The next day he confronted Mustafa, and they had a huge argument.

★

Suddenly my uncle let out a huge laugh, more like a roar, so loud that we all turned around to see what was going on, it didn't take long to work out that someone was telling him more stories at my expense.

"Aziz, don't let them get to you, everyone shits", Mustafa said with a huge grin.

We both laughed, and even though it was silly, his words relaxed me, and I stopped listening to the taunting that was still going on.

Chapter Fourteen

Cut From The Same Cloth

After a few drinks, we left to make our way back to Kyrenia, uncle Ilhan was relatively quiet with the occasional unprompted burst of laughter, as he continued to laugh about the 'shit boy' story.

"It is not that funny uncle," I said, but he was clearly ignoring me, and continued his ritual of laughing, every so often. Realising it was pointless trying to talk to him, I began to stare out of the car window to kill time.

"I can't wait to tell them. Dilan and Emir are going to love this story" uncle Ilhan said.

He had a look of such glee in his face. I couldn't help think, that had I not suggested the drink, that all of this would have been avoided.

"They already know about it uncle, so do most of the family". Though my uncle was just finding out about the story, by now, it was known by the majority of the family. However, I was sure uncle Ilhan would find someone that had never heard it before.

It was dark by the time we returned to the house, and as we entered, there were no lights on in the house, such that it looked as if no one was home.

As we made our way into the kitchen, we could see the light coming from the back of the house, and I realised that they were all sitting outside under the pergola.

As I approached, I could see the family all gathered around the table, which was made of a large slab of marble, held up by four painted white cement columns.

The marble table was beneath the pergola, and it was hard to see the metal structure through all the vine leaves and large bunches of grapes hanging down.

The grapes were so close that you would only simply have to lift your arm up to grab some. My grandparents were both very green fingered, and most of what they grew was the envy of all those around.

It was typical before summer to spray the growing grapes with pesticide to stop insects attacking the grapes before they were fully grown. The pesticide would leave a white mark on the grapes, and if you made the mistake of eating the grapes without washing the pesticide off, you had a good chance of getting violently ill.

One summer my grandparents noticed more, and more bunches of grapes were going missing. My grandparents decided to devise a plan by spraying new pesticide onto the grapes.

When you spray the pesticide on the grapes, the longer it is left, the easier it is to wash off, newly applied pesticide takes longer, and requires more care to clean. They sprayed the grapes, waited and watched.

When the next-door neighbours began complaining of stomach troubles, my grandfather went around to confront them. They immediately confessed to taking the grapes, and after the husband was told that his hands would be cut off if he ever stole again, the grapes were left alone for a while at least.

The pesticide plot occurred during one of our summer visits. Unfortunately, our grandparents had failed to inform us of their plans, so we were also taken ill from the poisoned grapes.

The plan backfired, as my grandmother was running around for days giving us medicine, and having to frequently clean the heavily used bathroom.

This wasn't the first time my grandfather had found thieves stealing from him.

For many people, they don't necessarily see it strictly as stealing. If you are close friends or family, then it is common to exchange produce with one another, I need tomatoes, while you need onions, etc.

This type of exchange is common, and it is not unheard of, that if you know someone, you could help yourself, and tell them afterwards what you had taken, only if there was enough produce available to go around.

When you don't know the person, or haven't had an exchange in the past, then this is considered theft.

On one such occasion, my grandfather was up a tree picking olives when he saw, in the distance two people standing over his tomato plants.

Not knowing who it was, my grandfather decided that he would go into stealth mode, and sneak up on the people.

As he got closer, he realised that it wasn't someone he knew, and realised the couple were stealing from him.

Enraged, he came up behind the man and struck him on the back of his head. The force of the slap was so hard, that the man immediately fell face first into the tomatoes.

The wife of the middle-aged man, saw her husband fall, and in a panic, ran to hide near a tree. When the man regained his composure, he got up and started to fight my elderly grandfather.

Though my grandfather was well into his 70s at the time, he was still fit, and very strong, and went about teaching this younger man a lesson that he wouldn't quickly forget.

Suddenly a large stone came hurtling past my grandfather's head, and hit the middle-aged man directly on his forehead. The man was instantly knocked out.

The wife in her panic to save her husband, had started to throw stones. Fortunately for my grandfather, her aim was not good, and every attempt didn't even come close to him.

At this point, the police had turned up to find my grandfather trying to remove the woman from up a tree, and her husband knocked out on the floor. My grandmother had seen the commotion in the distance, and had immediately called the police.

She had begun making her way up to where the action was, probably to join in with the middle-aged couple's lesson, however due to the size of their land this took my grandmother about fifteen minutes in her slow-paced 'running' to the scene of the crime.

By the time my grandmother arrived, the commotion was over, and the couple were being taken away.

The policemen arrested the woman, and her husband, and as they were getting into the car, they complained at their treatment by the hands of my grandfather.

No charges were ever brought against my grandfather due in part to him being well connected in Cyprus but also given that the couple was caught stealing, which is viewed as a serious crime.

As I got close to the marble table, my mother stood up, "Welcome home both of you, what took you so long?" my mother was clearly worried

"Your son wanted a drink because he was a mess after what happened with the Army" uncle Ilhan said. It was clearly a lie, but all eyes were on me to hear the real explanation.

"After being naturalised, uncle Ilhan and I agreed to go to Dede's café, so that I could buy uncle Ilhan a drink to thank him for taking me to Nicosia", my explanation seemed to annoy my mother.

"You could have called, I was worried about you" she responded.

After apologising, and telling her that it took longer than we had expected, I began to tell the story from beginning to end. When I was almost at the end of the story, uncle Ilhan piped up "Yeah, and your loving son has landed me in it, looks like I am going to have to do National Service".

I said that I had not known, and told everyone that uncle Ilhan had driven through the villages past the army bases just to taunt me.

As I was proclaiming my innocence, which was a lie, I looked over and saw my grandmother chuckling to herself. She knew that I was lying, but obviously thought it was all amusing.

I asked what everyone had been up to while we had been gone, and my father started telling us all that he had driven to the village where his family were from. He went there to visit the graves of his parents, and to pay his respects.

Both my father's parents had died long before I was born. My grandfather, on my father's side, had been a wealthy businessman, and owned a number of properties in both Cyprus and Turkey.

On their deaths, a family feud started, when all seven of the children began arguing over their inheritance.

My paternal grandparents were fair, and had divided up their entire estate equally between all of the children. However, the older brothers, and sisters had felt they were entitled to more.

At the time, my father was disgusted by his families' behaviour, and it took over twenty years for the rift that had formed, to heal.

My father, unlike my mother's family, had remained in Cyprus, except for one sister that lived in Australia.

My father had been really close to his family, but the death of his parents, and the greed of his siblings had resulted in them all drifting apart. In all the times we visited Cyprus, he never asked nor insisted that any of us visit his village or any member of his family.

Growing up, we knew we had a lot of cousins on my father's side of the family, but we had never met them and had no idea of how many there were nor their names.

Once my father told me that two of his brother's children were living in London, but it was more a side note, as he knew that it was unlikely I was going to meet them.

★

My father had actually inherited a twelve apartment complex in Nicosia, a house in Turkey and land in Cyprus. However, he had no interest in them, and after he learned that two of his brothers were taking the money generated from the properties, he just left them to it.

When my sister Sila found out, she was furious and asked our father why he would let his family steal from him. He only said, "I have all I need, a beautiful and amazing wife, amazing children, a great life and wonderful memories of my parents, what else could I want?"

He continued "My brothers and sisters are never content with what they have. If you gave then one hundred thousand dollars, they would want a million, they never appreciate what they have, and for that, I feel sorry for them, if they wish to steal from me, let them, my conscience is clear".

My sister dropped it after that, his explanation was one of the many reasons why we all had a tremendous amount of respect for our parents. He firmly believed in working hard for whatever he had, and he was more like his father, a shrewd, and successful business man.

"Before we go back Dad, I would like to come with you to visit our grandparent's graves to pay my respects," Sila said. I jumped in and said that I would also like to visit the graves.

Our request seemed to overwhelm him but before he could reply, our mother piped up.

"What is wrong with you two? Why would you want to visit the graves of two people you have never met, and if it were up to them, you would never have been born".

Our mother had a history with our paternal grandparents. Our father's parents were very proud of their son, and he could do wrong in their eyes, until he met our mother. Our mother's confidence seemed to intimidate them, and they did all they could to keep the young couple apart.

Though my father's parents disapproved, he was not willing to give up. He tried on a number of occasions for my mother, and his parents to get along, but once married, he realised that it was pointless, and decided that everyone would get on better with occasional visits.

Our mothers' response was more of frustration, and though they were dead, she was never one to forget.

"True my love, but it has been many years, and I never cared what they said. The moment I met you, you were my life", as he spoke our mother's demeanour changed and she became like an embarrassed teenager.

"Get a room" shouted Sila.

Even though my father's parents were unhappy with our mother over the years, they grew to respect her, and saw how happy she made our father. Before they passed away, they had been getting on a lot better.

"If you both want to go, I would be happy to take you", my father said. Both Sila and I nodded, and it was confirmed that we would go in two days' time.

I glanced over at my grandmother, who looked displeased. Though my mother's family would argue, they were extremely loyal to one another. My maternal grandparents took the dislike of my mother personally, and instantly hated them back.

Outside of family events, they would rarely see each other, and even when the relationship between my mother, and paternal grandparents had improved before their deaths, my maternal grandparents were less forgiving.

My mother's parents actually liked my father and did not seem to hold his family's issues against him. However, they would avoid talking about his family in front of him, as my grandfather would more than likely tell him what he thought of them otherwise.

*

By now it was getting really late, and one by one family members began going inside the house.

Eventually, it was just my mother, grandmother and I left at the table. Still thinking about the conversation with my father, my mother said: "So why do you and your sister want to see your grandparent's grave?"

"It is more for Dad, we never talk or know much about dad's family" I replied

"It is good for children to know where they come from, even if they are not good people," my grandmother said, clearly free to speak now my father had gone to bed

"Aziz, you don't know what it was like with that family, they hated me, as they felt I wasn't good enough for your father. However, if you and your sister want, you should learn more about them."

"I agree with you both, I just want to go for Dad" I replied.

"You are a good boy Aziz, you take after our side of the family," my grandmother said, as she grabbed my hand.

"Yes and Asim takes after your father's family," my mother said. With that, we all began to laugh.

"Right we all need to go to bed", said my mother, as she got up to begin clearing the table.

"I will do that," I said

"Thank you, Aziz, sleep well and see you tomorrow."

With that both my mother and grandmother kissed me, and went into the house to go to bed.

The table was full of bowls and cups, and it took a couple of trips to bring everything in.

As I wasn't tired, I began washing up.

A few minutes later I felt a hand touch my back, and turned around to see my grandmother standing behind me.

"Leave that Aziz, I will wash them in the morning."

"It is okay Nene, I suddenly don't feel tired" I replied

"You are a good boy Aziz, I know it is hard for your mother and father having you so far away from them."

"I know Nene, but I had to get away for a fresh start. I will go home, just not yet" I said

"That is good Aziz, it is good not to be too far from your family, it was always hard for your Dede and I having our family all over the world."

"I know Nene, but all of us have always loved seeing you both"

"I am glad everything went well with the Army Aziz," said my grandmother, a massive grin crossing her face.

"Sorry Nene, I know I shouldn't have done it, but he was taunting me the whole time."

"I know Aziz, it will be good for him to do it, and he always talks about how proud he is to be Turkish, now he can be fully Turkish," she said laughing.

"Private Ilhan has a nice ring to it" I agreed laughing.

"You are cut from the same cloth as me Aziz. Ilhan will one day learn that you are much smarter, and will always get the upper hand over him". With that, she kissed me on the cheek and walked off chuckling to herself.

Chapter Fifteen

Leave It To Ahmed

In the middle of the night I was woken up by a sharp pain in my throat, it seemed that my throat had become so dry, that it was beginning to hurt. As soon as I was awake, it quickly became apparent how hot the room had become, though the fan was at full speed, it was just circulating around the hot air.

I looked over, and even in this heat, both Dilan and Emir were peacefully asleep.

It was dark in the house, with all of the land surrounding the property and with it being set back so far from the street, there were no visible lights anywhere.

I decided to get a glass of water, as I made my way to the kitchen in the dark, I suddenly bashed my toe into the metal arm of one of the sofas in the living room.

"Shit", I said out loud, as I began hopping around the floor, in a lot of pain, screaming inside, trying not to wake everyone up.

Hopping into the kitchen, still nursing my toe, I immediately saw the silhouette of someone laying on the minder. It became clear from the loud snoring, that it was again my grandmother fast asleep.

I quietly grabbed a bottle of water and went back to the bedroom.

This was the second time that I had seen my grandmother sleeping on the minder. This is not entirely uncommon for a lot of people in summer sleep in the kitchen as it is generally cooler given the window had been open, and the fans have been on for most of the day, but it wasn't my grandmother's usual behaviour.

In the morning, I was awoken by one of my younger cousins, Yaffa, uncle Ilhan's daughter. She was only seven, and it quickly became apparent that my uncle had decided to let her run rampant in our room to wake us up.

Once in, she decided to climb up onto my bed, and with her first jump, she landed straight onto my stomach, immediately winding me.

"Be careful Yaffa" I said. Even though I was still winded, I grabbed Yaffa, and began tickling her until she was roaring with laughter.

"Please Abi" she screamed as I continue to tickle her.

"This will teach you to jump on me," I said laughing.

Yaffa was a natural beauty, and looked just like her mother. She was always so likeable, and full of energy, even when she was a baby.

The first time I ever saw her when she was first born, all I can remember was her smile, and how, even then, she was able to light up the room. She was a happy child, and was favoured by her father.

"Please Abi enough" she screamed, as I grabbed hold of her feet, and continued tickling her.

"Will you both stop", Dilan shouted, clearly being woken up by the noise.

"Chill out Dilan, Yaffa has just arrived".

Yaffa and I left and went to the kitchen, and found uncle Ilhan sitting at the kitchen table with my mother, father and sister.

"Where's Nene?" I asked.

"Outside with aunt Yildiz, preparing babutsa."

My aunt Yildiz, like her daughters, was a natural beauty, not only on the outside but also on the inside. She would often tell my uncle to stop when he was going too far. She was popular with all her in-laws, which is relatively rare in Turkish families, as normally the in-law is the person everyone in the family blames.

My aunt Mehtap once joked that if Ilhan and Yildiz ever broke up, the family would stay with her.

She was just kidding of course, but Yildiz definitely made my uncle a better man, and it was clear they were both deeply in love with each other.

There is a common misperception that arranged marriages are forced on people. Yildiz and Ilhan had been matched, but they went on a number of chaperoned dates, and only when their feelings started to grow, that it was then agreed they would marry.

Though Yildiz, and her family came to Cyprus to find her a husband, it was a big step for my uncle. When they agreed to get married, he knew that he would have to move, and start a new life in Germany. A big step, considering that he spoke no German.

Yaffa wanted to go outside, so I took her to see her mother. We found my grandmother, and aunt Yildiz seated at the marble table peeling the babutsa (also known as prickly pear).

"Aziz, so nice to see you", aunt Yildiz said as she got up to greet me.

"You too aunt, when did you arrive?"

"Yaffa and I came this morning. Unfortunately, Aylin, Hakan, Badia and Gizem had to stay behind with my parents because they still haven't finished the school term".

Yildiz was actually born in Germany, and all of her family still lived there. Unlike her husband, she represented the best of both cultures, and even the way she spoke was soft and polite.

"Oh that is a shame, how did little Yaffa get away with it? Maybe we should send her back" I said, tickling Yaffa.

"Yaffa got permission from her school. She is doing very well at school, and is the top of her class" my aunt said laughing, but clearly proud.

"Ahhh, she must take after you aunt Yildiz then," I said laughing

"I hear the naturalisation went well, and that Ilhan is going to now have to do national service."

"That was his own fault, aunty, he was showing off in front of the general, and he got caught out."

Yildiz began laughing as she said, "He can't help himself."

Babutsa is the fruit from the native cactus, and found all over Cyprus. The fruit once peeled, is sweet, quite different in texture, and is very popular with people all over Cyprus.

Not paying much attention, I decided to grab a babutsa not realising it, but I had reached into the bowl of unpeeled fruits.

215

"No Aziz, you need to wear gloves" my grandmother screamed.

Unfortunately, my grandmother's warning was too late. Though the fruit is delicious, to get to it, you have to get past the small prickly spikes, which are so small that they go easily into the skin, thus giving its name, prickly pear.

"Bloody hell" I shouted. My right hand was now covered in small spikes, and with every movement, I could feel the spikes going deeper into my hand.

My mother spent an hour with a magnifying glass and tweezers removing most of the spikes, but it took days for me to be free of them.

The whole time my mother was pulling them out she was calling me an idiot and that I should have known better, which was true, I should have.

Everyone decided to head to the beach but with my grandmother not being able to leave the house, my mother and I decided to stay behind to keep her company.

As soon as everyone had left, I found out that my grandmother's friends were coming around to take coffee.

My mother said that I did not have to sit with them, but I should come out and at least greet them when they arrived. Had I known that this was happening, I would have gone to the beach.

Thirty minutes later I could hear the old ladies arriving. They decided to take the coffee in the shade under the pergola, and when I went out to greet them, it was clear to see they were a little uncomfortable.

I had been to Cyprus a lot growing up, and had met them all a number of times, some of them were even family, however on one family trip I embarrassed myself, and it was clear to see they hadn't forgotten.

My parents, sister, brother, and I had a trip to Cyprus when I was eleven years old. On a trip to the beach at the start of our trip, I spent the whole day in the sea. My mother kept telling me to get out of the water, but whenever anyone came near, I would simply swim away, to avoid being captured. The only time I left the water, was to go and grab food and then run straight back into the sea.

When it was time to go home, I started to feel really strange, and quickly discovered that I had chronic diarrhoea. On the drive home, we had to stop about fifteen times, in order for me to avoid any mishaps in the car.

With each stop, my grandfather would shout "For God's sake, we are never going to get home at this rate"

That night I spent more time on the toilet than in bed, I wasn't sure how so much was coming out of me as I had been to the bathroom so many times.

I remember analysing the entire bathroom, the patterns in the tiles, and the excess grout on the tiles that my grandparents had never scrapped off. I quickly knew every part of that bathroom, spending so much time in there.

My family immediately became worried when diarrhoea turned into blood the next morning. My grandfather, feeling a little guilty for being so impatient with me the day before, insisted that I was taken to the hospital.

My grandfather drove me, my mother, and father to the hospital, with my grandmother staying behind to look after my younger siblings. When we arrived at the hospital, I was seen immediately as my grandfather made such a huge scene.

Everyone was worried, and even though I was somewhat delirious, I remember their concern, and my mother constantly touching my head.

"Get someone now! If anything happens to my grandson, I will kill you all" my grandfather said threatening the young nurse who was close to the waiting area.

"Don't worry uncle, we will look after him" the nurse said reassuringly.

After a short time, I was seen by a doctor, and I was diagnosed with having severe sunstroke. I was given a concoction of pills and injections and released from the hospital. The next two weeks were a blur, being bedridden and heavily medicated.

The day my grandmother's friends came around for coffee, my mother had been concerned that I had been cooped up, and had believed that I needed fresh air. After my bath, she decided to move my bed to the veranda.

As it was a hot day, the women had gathered on the veranda with me.

When my mother returned from making coffee, and bring the snacks, she found the ladies with their backs to me, pretending to make small talk about the plants in my grandmother's garden.

My mother found me on top of the covers, completely naked fast asleep. In my delirious state, I had removed my clothes to combat the heat.

My mother quickly threw a sheet over me, and then moved the bed back inside the house to avoid further embarrassment.

My mother told my grandmother what happened once her friends had left. My grandmother found the story amusing and said "why were they so embarrassed though? Surely they have husbands and children, have they not seen a naked child before, I don't know why they were acting like it is a big shock!"

Coffee mornings were common place with Turkish women, with them often meeting daily to socialise.

These coffee mornings were where you would find out the gossip from the village, and the comments could often be brutal about people they are acquainted with, even close friends of the family.

It was typical of them to start the sentences with, "you know me, I don't like to talk bad about people, but...." which often concluded with some titbit of gossip.

For an outsider, these coffee mornings looked innocent enough, but they were just a cover to gossip, and boast.

When they are not gossiping, they will brag about family, and the latest developments. The preference was always to talk about family members overseas, as you can embellish the truth a little more freely, as it is likely no one knows what is true, and what is fiction.

The men do exactly the same thing, with less discretion in large groups in the café. Fights would often occur when someone was gossiping, usually not realising that the person they were talking about was close by.

★

Despite my naked encounter with the ladies being a long time ago, every time I saw them, there was always a short moment of awkwardness.

"Welcome aunts," I said, as I kissed each of the old ladies' cheeks in turn.

"So nice to see you, Aziz, I hear from your grandmother you are doing well," one of them said.

"He is doing very well, he has been promoted 3 times in the last year alone, and is beating off the women in London with a stick," my grandmother said. She was naturally proud, but with Turkish women, there was always an element of one-upmanship.

"That is so good, you should go see my grandson Aziz, he is a successful doctor in London", said one of the old ladies.

I actually knew her grandson, he was a good man, but was actually a nurse, a fact his grandmother had clearly omitted.

"I have actually seen him recently aunt Fingun, he is doing very well," I said making the old lady beam with pride.

I generally avoided spending too much time at these types of gatherings preferring to avoid the gossip and boasting.

"Did you hear about Mohammed in the village?" one of the women asked, "No, what has happened?" my grandmother said.

"You know that his mother died, well his family were seen fighting in the street over their inheritance."

"They should be ashamed of themselves," My grandmother said, thought she did not seem surprised. As she said it, a number of the old woman nodded in agreement.

★

A lot of the people on the island are financially comfortable, but not necessarily wealthy. They typically own their own homes but have to keep animals, and work to pay the bills.

Though families are close, often when money is involved, fighting starts. Not all behave this way, but there is a proportion that distrust one another.

"If my children acted like that, I would rather give it to the Greeks than them," one of the ladies said.

"I would rather leave it to my nephew in Nicosia, he is hard working, and at least I know he would appreciate it" another commented.

"God, I would hope that my family would have more respect for me, and respect our wishes," one of other the ladies said.

"Yes I know what you mean, that is why Mustafa and I decided to leave it all to Ahmed," my grandmother said.

With that, the ladies roared with laughter, for everyone knew that Ahmed was the husband of my aunt Mehtap, and the person my grandfather liked least in the family.

Chapter Sixteen

For The Love Of Figs

The following day, my father reminded us about going to visit his parent's grave. "You really don't have to go if you don't want to", my father said. He was trying not to be pushy but, it was clear that he would have been disappointed if we had said no.

Our mother who was sitting at the table was waiting for our reaction.

"Of course, we want to go dad" I replied. I could see the disappointment on my mother's face as soon as I had said it.

"God that sounds like fun" uncle Ilhan replied, but my father just ignored him.

"Okay then, Aziz and Sila, we will need to leave soon. Sila, go have a shower," my father said. Usually, Sila would give some sort of backchat about why does it have to be her first, but on this occasion, she just got up and went to the bathroom.

I had my shower, and went back to wait with my father. Sila was taking ages doing her hair.

"Sila can you hurry up, we are not going to a beauty pageant" my father shouted.

"I am coming, God, you guys are so impatient" Sila shouted back.

Some minutes later, and after arguing about who would sit in the front, we eventually got into the Volvo to drive to my father's village.

It was strange, that even though I was in my late twenties, when around my siblings, we always seemed to behave like we were still teenagers.

★

My father's village was close to the border in the northern part of Famagusta. For the entire journey, my father was telling stories of his parents, what they were like and what it was like for him growing up.

Though you could tell at times it was a little emotional for him, as it had been so long ago, he kept his composure.

"I see so much of my mother in you Sila," my father said.

"Oh great, mum said she was awful", Sila remarked. She was known for speaking before she thinks, but this time it was a little raw.

"My parents were never kind to your mother Sila, and that was my fault for never fully resolving it, but they were not bad people, just misguided when it came to your mother."

"Oh my god, look at that", I said, partly changing the subject, but also pointing to the sight before us.

Next to us was an old Renault 5, with at least twelve people crammed inside. All you could see were arms and faces squashed against the windows of the car.

"So bloody dangerous", my father said laughing, "it is like that are trying to play twister in the car."

The car was so full that it was clearly slowing down the vehicle, the sheer weight of the people was making them drive at a slow 30 mph on a 70 mph motorway.

After laughing, my father suddenly got serious and said: "I want us to first go just outside Famagusta, as there is something I want to show you both". We both nodded, still looking back at the bloated car, chuckling.

✫

We arrived in Famagusta, and although I had been before, I had forgotten just had beautiful it was; with its golden beaches and the sun beating down, it was like a picture found on a holiday postcard. As we approached the centre of town, we assumed we had arrived when the car began to slow down, but my father kept driving through the heart of the city.

We were on the road, that was relatively quiet that ran alongside the sea. On one side you had the sea for miles, and on the other side, relatively untouched land, just a few apartment buildings or small villas scattered here and there.

The road was so quiet, and for most of the journey we were the only car on the road.

When we came up to an open area near the beach, my father pulled over, and parked on a small dirt road, which was clearly well used given the tyre marks indented on the ground.

Though we were still in Northern Cyprus, our father had taken us right up to the border, the border which separates the Turkish Northern Cyprus from the Greek Southern Cyprus. The border itself is patrolled by the United Nations, and is known as the Green Line.

"That is the town of Varosha" he said as he pointed to where derelict buildings could be seen behind a metal fence.

"I used to go to Varosha often as a child, and it was once a huge tourist town. After the 1974 war, neither the Turkish nor Greek government could settle on who should own the town. As a result, it is now part of the Green Line, and no civilians are allowed to enter".

Our father went on to explain that during the war, people had fled for their lives. As no civilians were allowed to enter, the town remained untouched, with people's money still in their houses, unmade beds, almost a time capsule from the 1970s.

It was sad to see the buildings decaying, and that so long after the war, that there still is no resolution to its sovereignty. We stared at this ghost city for some time until our father ushered us back to the car to continue our visit to our father's childhood village.

★

"We are here," our father said, pointing to a few scattered houses in the distance. A lot of the villages were small, typically houses were one or two storeys high, with the main square of the village being the most populated areas.

Soon after we passed the welcome sign to the village, my father began slowing down.

"Wow, who is that?" Sila asked pointing to a man on the veranda of the house closest to us.

"That looks like it is your first cousin Omer," my father said. Immediately we both started laughing, Sila was not amused.

"Wow, you took getting close to the family too literally Sila," I said.

"Well, how was I to know! Actually now I can see him clearer, he is not that good looking" Sila said clearly trying to play down her earlier comment.

Once the car engine was turned off, my father said: "This house used to belong to your grandfather, it is now owned by my sister, your aunt."

As we walked up to the gate, the house looked like it hadn't been maintained in years. It was a two-storey property, and the garden faced the beach, and in its day, it must have been beautiful.

There was a small path leading up to the house, and either side of the path was full of plants. There was a strong smell of Jasmine in the air, and as we opened the rusty gate, it was easy to see that paint on the house, at one-time was yellow, was now peeling off, and the walls had a few holes in them.

As we got closer to the veranda, a short fat lady came out to greet us calling "Welcome brother, nephew, niece, it is so nice to see you".

After greeting us, we went to the veranda.

"Get up you lazy bastard," she said as she kicked the young man. We realised that he had actually been listening to a CD Walkman, and didn't hear our arrival or his mother's insults until she kicked him.

"I am so glad to finally meet you both, I am your aunt Irmak, and this is one of my sons Omer, say hello Omer", Omer jumped up and welcomed us.

"Aziz, Sila I have so many pictures of you both. Your father would send them to me when you were growing up, I have kept every one of them" aunt Irmak said as she led us into her home.

Although the house, and furniture looked old, you could tell it was clean, and that Irmak was very house proud.

"Would you like coffee, tea, a cold drink?" Irmak asked as she led us through the house to the garden which faced the sea.

Once we were settled, Omer came outside with plates of food, one filled with cut watermelon and another of Baklava, a sweet filo pastry filled with pistachio nuts and soaked in syrup. Another was full of Kadayif, a sweet wheat dessert that looks like a breakfast cereal, and finally a large bowl of Muhallebi, a creamy pudding topped with rose water.

"Please family, eat," Omer said as he placed the food in front of us.

★

The sight and the rose smell of the Muhallebi brought back more memories from my youth. We had gone to Nicosia for a day trip, and as we walked around the shops in the heat, I spotted a man selling ice cream.

I was so excited, as I had always loved ice cream growing up, and the sight of the man, made me plead with my parents to buy me some.

Turkish ice cream, known as Dondurma, is very different to Western ice creams, as it has two additional ingredients known as mastic and salep.

Mastic is extracted from the mastic tree, and once dried forms into brittle pieces that look like little stones.

Mastic, also known as Arabic gum, is used in a lot of Turkish recipes, and it is common for people to chew on the mastic as it softens into a sort of chewing gum.

The addition of the mastic to the ice cream makes the ice cream chewy, and almost elasticated when stretched.

I always loved Dondurma, so as soon as my parents agreed, my cousin Dilan, and I went rushing over to place our order.

The ice cream seller had four flavours, Chocolate, Strawberry, Mint and Vanilla. My favourite fruit, and flavour had always been strawberry, so naturally, I ordered strawberry.

Once we had placed our order, the ice cream seller did his little show of turning the ice cream upside down over our heads, and pretending to hand the cone to us, only to take it away again.

Though Dilan and I were pretending to play along, we really just wanted our ice cream.

As I walked back to my parents, I started to lick my ice cream.

"This isn't strawberry", I said to my parents, close to tears. The strawberry coloured ice cream was actually rose flavoured, a flavour that even to this day, I am unable to consume.

My family, however, thought it was highly amusing and my mother had the pleasure of eating the ice cream.

★

"I am so sorry to hear about your grandfather," aunt Irmak said as she came back with the drinks.

"Thank you, he had a good long life though", I replied.

"I hear you live in London Aziz," Omer said. He then went on to say this two of his older brothers lived in London, and that he was planning to go over when he was 21, once he had finished university.

"That is really good Omer, what are you studying?" I replied. Before he could respond aunt Irmak began speaking to our father, making it hard to hear.

"I am so happy to see you brother, it has been so long," she said.

"Yes, the last time was when Ercan died. Such a hard time" my father replied.

Over two years ago, while I was still living in Los Angeles, our father had to fly out to Cyprus as his brother-in-law, Ercan had tragically died of cancer.

"Yes, it hasn't gotten any easier, I still miss him," aunt Irmak said as she began to cry. My father immediately jumped up to go and console her.

For some Cypriots, no matter the age, once their partner dies they typically remain widowed, and will not look for another relationship. My father told us once a while ago that aunt Irmak was very lonely.

After catching up with her for over an hour, and being shown many old pictures of both Sila, Asim and me that my father had sent, we were informed that aunt Irmak was going to come with us to the cemetery. After saying goodbye to Omer, we all got back into the car.

The cemetery was only a short drive away; as with most village cemeteries, you could see the same family name on many of the gravestones that we passed.

When we reached the plot, there were two modest name stones with our paternal grandparent's names etched on them. Although they were relatively well maintained, my father immediately began ripping weeds from the ground around the headstone.

Both graves were inside a well-constructed metal fence, and to rip the weeds from the ground, my father had to lean right over the fence, almost falling in.

"I am so sorry brother, I come often, but it is hard with looking after the family and the house," aunt Irmak said.

"Don't be silly, I rarely come, and it is clear you do all you can".

"Last time I came here, as it had been so long, I was so emotional that I spent the whole time crying," my father said, as soon as he had said it, Sila linked arms with our father.

Turkish people are generally very family orientated, and are rarely ever forgotten about. Even the nasty and unkind relatives are spoken about in stories, passed down through the generations.

"Is there anything I can do to help you Irmak?" my father said.

"Brother you already do so much for my family and me, the money you send us, and give us from the properties, has meant all of my children, and I live so well."

Sila and I immediately looked over at each other. We were surprised, we hadn't realised that our father was sending money over to Cyprus, and more importantly was our mother aware?

Though we were surprised, it was evident to see why he was doing it. This woman was now bringing up her family, with insufficient state support, and as is common with Turkish families, everyone helps out.

"You are the best of us brother, all of the others did not care what happened to me," aunt Irmak said, referring to my father's other siblings.

"Let's not worry about them, all that matters is that you are okay" he replied.

"It is such a shame how our parents treated your wife. For so many years they lost out on so much, for no reason," aunt Irmak said. It surprised both Sila and me that aunt Irmak mentioned her parents, and our mother's relationship.

"I know Irmak, but it is the past now, and hopefully we will all be reunited in the afterlife" my father replied

Sila and I looked at each other, and tried not to laugh. We could imagine our mother's reaction to death, and having to spend eternity with her in-laws.

Once we paid our respects to our grandparents, we drove aunt Irmak back to her house. When we arrived, we could see three other people on the veranda; we later found out that they were my father's older brothers Adil, Cemal and Erol.

My father told us to stay in the car as he walked my aunt to the veranda. After speaking to his brothers for a brief while, we saw my aunt hugging my father for a long time. Once they broke the embrace, it was clear that she had been crying.

Once our father was back in the car, Sila asked: "Why didn't you want us to meet them, Dad?"

"They are not good people Sila and I don't want my family to have anything to do with them. I am polite to them, but after what they have done, I don't want them to be part of our lives".

As we waved goodbye to our aunt and began driving back to Kyrenia, my father began opening up about all the things they had done, during and after his parent's death.

They were clearly greedy and selfish, and though my father was respectful, it was clear that he disliked all of his three brothers and two of his three sisters.

"I never want you to become like this. I know you all fight, but it is important you all look out for each other, even Asim" my father said.

"For the love of figs, I am not being lumbered with Asim," Sila said, laughing.

Chapter Seventeen

Like Baklava

When we arrived back to the house, all of the family were outside busy preparing dinner. Uncle Ilhan, and uncle Mehmet had used some bricks to make a makeshift barbecue, and next to them were trays of skewered meat ready to be cooked.

On the marble table, next to the barbecue were mountains of food; pitta bread, salad, yoghurt and cheese. It was clear that in our absence the family had been busy preparing a big meal.

"Welcome back, did you manage to connect with your grandparents," our mother said, with a sarcastic tone in her voice.

"Actually mum, it was nice, we got to meet aunt Irmak, she seemed nice" I replied.

"Oh nice, how is Irmak? I haven't seen her in years."

"Well you could come next time my love", our father said clearly trying to get our mother to pay more interest in his family, but she wasn't having any of it.

"We are not here on holiday" my mother quickly replied.

Apparently bored and wanting to get up to mischief, Dilan blurted out "Do you remember when you shaved your pubes, Aziz?"

With those words, everyone stopped what they were doing to listen to Dilan.

"He saw an evil spirit, and got scared. The next day we all went to the mosque, but Aziz wasn't aware, that I had asked uncle Ozturk to be in on the joke. He told him to shave off his pubes to protect himself from bad spirits."

As soon as Dilan had finished the story, everyone began roaring with laughter. The story Dilan was telling, wasn't the whole thing, clearly not telling everyone how he too, had been scared.

We had all been sleeping on the roof of our grandparent's house. A few of our distant cousins from the village came to stay at the house in Kyrenia, so we decided to start telling ghost stories, or 'cins' as they are known, to scare one another. On by one, we told our stories, and with each one, they were getting worse and darker, with each person trying to outdo the other. The problem was that it was dark on top of the roof, and the stories were unnerving everyone, even though no one wanted to admit it.

Dilan started telling a story about a wolf that stole the spirits of people for its evil dead owner. The wolf would roam at night looking for unsuspecting souls.

As soon as the story was finished, we heard a large rustling sound coming from the plants next to the house. We all rushed over to the side of the roof to investigate.

We looked down to see what seemed like a wolf, looking up at us growling. Everyone swore it was a wolf, which was strange, as there are no wolves on the island.

We all got freaked out, and began panicking whether there was truth in the story, Dilan included. During the commotion, we saw our grandparent's black Labrador came running to our aid, and started to attack the so-called wolf. After a lot of growling, and biting, the 'wolf' finally retreated.

Still freaked out, we all climbed down the ladder, and went into the house. Unnerved, Dilan remembered that our grandparents had a Koran in their bedroom, so we snuck in to room to take it. Once he had the Koran, we went into the bathroom to wash, and began reading prayers, which seemed to calm everyone, like the words were repealing any evil spirits close by.

The next day as we told our grandfather, he just laughed a lot and said: "Don't be so stupid, there are no wolves in Cyprus, you are starting to sound like my crazy mother."

Even to this day, whenever I think back to that story, and hear of someone being radicalised, I always remember how easily groups can influence one another.

A lot of Islamic cultures talk of the devil, and evil spirits, and people are fearful, so it is easy to see how these fears can be taken advantage of.

We decided that we would go to the mosque, and be totally cleansed. When we arrived my grandmother's cousin, Ozturk was outside, and when he greeted us, Dilan went on to tell him what happened to us.

"Oh that is not good, that sounds like an evil spirit to me," Ozturk said, he had a solemn look, and given he was a priest, we all started to get worried.

"The best thing to do is to totally purify yourself, when you go home, shave off all your pubic hair, and wash four times," he said.

After praying at the mosque, we all rushed back, and I did exactly what the priest had told me to do.

"Did you do it?" Dilan said

"Yes, just finished", with that Emir and Dilan erupted with laughter. I hadn't realised that earlier in the day, Dilan had seen Ozturk at the village shop, and he had asked him to play along with his prank.

Luckily, I was only twelve at the time, so didn't have a lot to shave off, however for weeks I was scratching my groin, every time remembering the prank played on me.

Dilan told everyone immediately, and my grandparents, though trying to be serious, and saying that it was bad, couldn't resist, and ended up laughing at what had happened.

It was years later that we found out that the so-called 'wolf' was actually an Alsatian dog that was owned by someone that lived further up the mountain. In the end, it was my grandmother that got revenge on the dog.

The dog kept on escaping, and killing peoples' animals. At a family event, we were talking about my aunt's new Persian cat, when my grandmother began laughing for no reason.

"Do you remember that wolf dog?"

"Yes Nene, but it was more like a donkey than a dog."

"Well I killed it," she said, laughing uncontrollably, while we all looked at her in shock.

She went on to explain that the dog had killed three of her chickens, so she took action. She cut up and cooked a sponge in animal fat, and oil. That night she locked up her dog inside the house, and left the cooked sponge outside near the kitchen door for the intruder.

During the night, the dog came, and ate the sponge. A week later, her neighbour told her that the dog was found dead. The sponge, once consumed, had expanded in the dog's stomach making it unable to eat.

My grandmother didn't necessarily do it to be cruel, even though she did find the story funny, it was more out of necessity. She told us that she had asked the owners a number of times to keep the dog tied up, but when it kept on killing animals, which was affecting people's livelihoods, she wasn't going to sit around, and do nothing.

Once she finished her story, we all just sat there stunned in silence, while my grandmother still continued laughing.

After we had finished the barbecue feast, my grandmother told everyone that a storm was coming, and that we should close all of the windows, and put blankets on the beds.

One by one, family members left the house, and once all the plates and cups were washed, Dilan, Emir and I went to bed.

"God did you see how much Ilhan was eating," Dilan said.

"It was like he wanted to make sure he got back the kilo of meat he paid for," Emir said laughing

We spoke for a little while and soon all feel asleep. In all our joking around, we had forgotten two things - the blankets, and the window.

I was woken up in the early hours of the morning shivering. The temperature had suddenly dropped, but when I went to the cupboard to get a blanket, it seemed that Emir and Dilan had beaten me to it, and taken all of the blankets, luckily though, they had closed the window. All that was left for me to use was my grandmother's heavy yorgan.

The yorgan is a Turkish type of throw. Traditionally they would place sheep's wool inside padded silk, and then sew it onto layers of sheets. Though they were perfect in winter for keeping in the warmth, they were extremely heavy.

In my childhood, I often remember being trapped under a yorgan all night, unable to move from the sheer weight, like a tightly wrapped burrito. I put the yorgan on my bed and decided to go, and get a drink of water before going back to sleep.

★

As soon as I walked into the kitchen, I saw my grandmother asleep again on the minder. The kitchen was cold, and she had no covers on her. I went into her bedroom to get some blankets, and when I returned, I gently put the blanket over her.

"What are you doing," my grandmother said, half asleep.

"You were asleep on the minder Nene, I was just putting a blanket to cover you, and it is getting cold."

"Thank you Aziz", she said as she began to sit up.

"Why are you not sleeping in your bed Nene," I asked

"I can't sleep in there, it reminds me too much of Mustafa."

"Do you want us to change rooms Nene? Dilan, Emir and I can stay in there if you prefer."

"Thank you Aziz, but I can't sleep in any bed, as it feels empty without your grandfather."

My grandmother always had this hard demeanour about her, so it was surprising to hear her speak like this. My grandparents would often put on 'shows' for us, and it would typically involve my grandmother doing some sort of housework, and our grandfather sneaking up behind her to poke and tickle her. She would turn around and beat him, and we would roll around the floor laughing.

They would often get into huge arguments, and if someone happened to be passing by, you would think that someone had been killed from the noise.

"You know that we both love you very much," my grandmother said out loud. It took me by surprise, as I had never heard her use the word love in that context before.

"I know you do Nene" I replied

"No Aziz, Dede too. He was always tough on you because you were the eldest grandson, but he was very proud, and he loved you very much."

"I know he loved me Nene, but he always seemed to be angry with me". As my grandfather would often shout at only me when my cousins had also been involved in our antics.

"I know, but he always told me that you, and he are very much alike."

"Dede and I alike?" I must have looked confused.

"Yes, he always said that you were a better version of him, and he wanted to make sure you didn't make the same mistakes as him" my grandmother sincerity, and admissions surprised me.

"You are kind, smart, and are a great man, we are all very proud of you".

With that my grandmother leant over, and began to hug me. It was strange to be embraced by a person that wasn't used to it but being emotional, she must have felt compelled.

My grandmother started to tell me some stories about my grandfather. It was a side of my grandfather that I had never seen before. One story made me laugh so loud that I almost woke up the house.

We all knew my grandfather loved animals, although he was happy to look after them, but when it came to killing them, he would send in my grandmother.

On one occasion a number of little chicks were born, and he kept them in a hutch at the back of the property. My grandfather would go feed them, and look after them two or three times a day.

One of the chicks was ill, and no matter what my grandfather did, the poor little chick only got sicker. After my grandmother had protested that the chick would likely infect the healthy chicks, my grandmother insisted that he kill the chick.

All day he kept on going in and out of the house, clearly putting off having to do it.

After my grandmother had shouted at him for the hundredth time, he went out to get the task done. He decided that he couldn't watch this poor creature die, so he made a contraption using a bottle and string to effectively choke the chick. Everything was ready, he took the chick out of the hutch, and tried to prepare himself for the task at hand.

While pacing, a large bird suddenly swooped down, and grabbed the little chick. Though my grandfather must have been relieved, he was shouting at the thief that had stolen one of his animals.

I am not sure why, but I suddenly blurted out to my grandmother that Ayla was getting married. I hadn't told anyone in the family yet about it.

"One of my friends from Los Angles was over in London, and he said that he saw one of Ayla's brothers in a bar, in which he told him that she was getting married."

"Ah she is tricking another man into marrying her, only to leave them" my grandmother replied.

I explained that the brother had told my friend that while she had been in Africa, she had met a German doctor, and that they fell deeply in love. They had been dating ever since, which by now was a couple of years, and that she was now ready to settle down.

"How do you feel about that?" my grandmother asked

"Good luck to her, but to honest, I think she is a coward. If she didn't want to marry me, she should have spoken to me before the wedding, but now I am glad that it ended."

"Good for you Aziz, that bitch doesn't deserve someone like you."

Though it had been some time, hearing that Ayla was getting married, strangely felt like that chapter was finally over.

"Does that mean you are going back to Los Angeles now Aziz? Especially with what is wrong with your father."

The sheer look of shock on my face, my grandmother immediately realised she had said something she was not meant to.

"Aziz I am so sorry, please speak to your mother, I shouldn't have said anything."

"Please Nene, tell me, I just want to know."

My grandmother went on to explain that my father was diagnosed with cancer, and he had been told that he had a 50% survival rate. She said that my mother was falling apart, but she didn't want her children to know.

My father was undergoing treatment but wanted to come to Cyprus in case it was his last time.

Thinking back to aunt Irmak's house, and the way she was crying, it was clear that he must have told her about his diagnosis. That was probably also why he didn't want us to get out of the car.

I also thought back to my aunt Lale's reaction to me when I first saw her, she would have definitely known as she was close with my mother.

"Why did no one tell me Nene?" I said I could feel the tears welling up in my eyes.

"Your mother didn't want to worry you all, and she said that she didn't want you to come back home, just because of this."

"I know he will be okay Nene, but what if he isn't? Am I losing time with him?"

"Don't think like that Aziz, he will get better."

My grandmother told me to go to bed and to try to get some sleep before everyone woke. I nodded, but I knew, given what I had just learnt, I wouldn't be getting much sleep.

Though I could understand why my parents were protecting us, I still wanted to know to be able to make my own decisions.

"Thank you, Nene, it was nice to talk to you about Dede," I said as I kissed her goodnight.

"Aziz, please don't worry about your father, God is watching him, he is a good man and will be all right."

"I hope so Nene."

"One last thing Aziz, I just wanted you to know that though your Dede could be tough, he was also like Baklava, full of sweet layers, and don't ever forget that he loved you very much".

Chapter Eighteen

How Lucky

★ ★ ★

I hardly slept the rest of the night, my mind racing thinking about my father. My grandmother was unable to give me that many details, what type of cancer it was, what was the treatment, I had so many unanswered questions.

Eventually deciding that I was too awake to sleep, I decided to get up, and go outside. I remembered seeing a packet of cigarettes in Dilan's bag, so I took one.

I kept on thinking about my parents. I always knew that my parents would die at some point, but he was too young; I couldn't help it, but I began to sob uncontrollably.

Once I had finished the cigarette, I finally pulled myself together, and made my way back into the house

"Why aren't you sleeping Aziz?" my grandmother called from the kitchen

"I just couldn't sleep", I said as I joined her. It was evident my grandmother had been up for a while as she was rolling out pastry on the table.

"Aziz, I hope it is not because of what I said about your father," she said.

"What about your father?" my mother asked as she had walked into the kitchen, clearly catching the end of the sentence.

"It is nothing" I replied.

"What is wrong with you Aziz, you have a face like a slapped arse?" my mother said in her usual style.

"He knows, I am so sorry, I made a mistake last night," my grandmother said.

★

My mother just sat down on the minder, and it was as someone had punched her in the stomach.

"Mum why didn't you tell me", before I could go on, my grandmother jumped in, "You both need to speak, go into my bedroom for privacy."

I followed my mother but noticed, everything was different about her; she wasn't walking in her usual confident way, it wasn't the mother I was used to, it was unnerving me.

"What is wrong with Dad? Please tell me" I said once we had reached the room.

"Your father has cancer. He has type four kidney cancer, but they believe there is secondary cancer elsewhere. They removed a tumour, but your father has to undergo chemotherapy."

"Oh my God Mum, is he going to be okay?"

My mother suddenly went quiet, and she sat on the bed, with her head in her hands.

"Mum please tell me what is going on."

"I don't know, but I'm scared," she said, I sat next to her and put my arm around her.

"Mum, he is going to be okay, I am sure of it", I had so many questions, but seeing my mother like this, I was more worried about her.

"I really hope so Aziz" with that she turned, and all I could see were huge tears rolling down her face. Seeing my mother like this disturbed me, she was a strong woman and kept us together, and strong.

Suddenly the door opened and in walked Dilan coming to return some of the blankets from the night before. Seeing my mother crying like this, and me consoling her, clearly worried him.

"What's going on?" Dilan rushed over, and knelt down next to my mother's legs, and starting hugging her.

My mother began to explain to Dilan about my father, the whole time he looked in shock, and kept on saying no, as the tears rolled down his face.

I wanted to cry, but seeing my mother and cousin crying stopped me, I felt I had to be strong for them.

After crying for a while, my mother begged us to act normal, and not to say anything to my father. We both reluctantly agreed.

★

When I booked the flight out to Cyprus, I was only able to book 1 week off from work, and my return to London was scheduled for the following day. At breakfast, my mother reminded everyone that I was leaving.

"I know we are meant to be mourning, but we could still go to the beach, as long as we wear black", Emir said, half joking

"I think it is a good idea" I replied, everyone, seemed surprised as it was somewhat out of character for me to go along with such plans.

"Ask Serdar in the village, he has a 7 seater that we could use," my grandmother said.

★

About an hour later, the 7 seater vehicle, Volvo and Volkswagen were packed as if we were moving to the beach. There was so much stuff that they were all bursting at the seams. Except for the drivers, all of the passengers had stuff on their legs and laps. Everyone began saying goodbye to my grandmother who was planning to spend the day cleaning.

Despite arguing, my mother, and one of my aunts were also forced to go to the beach by my grandmother.

"I don't need you around my feet all day" my grandmother said, as she ashered them out of the door.

When my aunt Lale climbed into the 7 seater, I laughed. Seeing her large rear end squeezing into the small van, it reminded me of the little car on the motorway we had seen with my father.

I drove the old Volkswagen again, which gave my uncle Ilhan great pleasure, knowing that I would have to drive that old heap of a vehicle. Dilan, Emir, Sila and Sevda all decided to come with me, and we spoke and laughed the whole way down to the beach.

"How's the hunt going Sevda?" Dilan asked

"Oh my god, I know I want a Turkish husband, but seriously, I was introduced to a man in his forties! What was worse was the fact that his family believed that I was lucky he considered me" Sevda replied

"Sevda you need to go with the white guy, get with a guy that actually likes you," Dilan replied.

"Shut up Dilan, I know I will find someone" she snapped

Once we arrived at the beach, my uncle Ilhan told us all to follow him, as he knew the perfect spot.

In Cyprus, the coastline is a mixture of golden sandy, and rocky beaches. Kyrenia had rockier beaches. However the local authority had cleared one, and it was now a beautiful golden sand beach, popular with both tourists and locals. The beach was busy, but we immediately began to settle in, by unpacking our towels, food, drinks, and whatever else everyone decided to bring with them.

"What the hell are they looking at", said uncle Ilhan, responding to the strange looks we were getting from the tourists on the beach.

At the time, he was busy digging a hole in the sand near the water's edge. Once he dug the hole, he placed both of the watermelons inside, so only half of it could be seen.

Though he was getting strange looks, this is an old technique for ensuring that the watermelon remains cold, as the water washes over to it. The beach was full of both tourists, and locals, all out worshiping the sun. Young and old, everyone had swimwear on, that was way too revealing.

I knew my mother was trying to act normal when a large woman walked past with a small swimming costume on, but she couldn't help remarking "What does she think she looks like?"

Arriving at the beach brought back a lot of memories of my grandfather, he loved the beach, and sea and whenever we came to visit he would take us there often.

The only issue with my grandfather was that he would get bored really quickly, and was far too restless. No sooner had we arrived anywhere, we were back in the car.

My grandmother was the opposite, as long as she had shade, and someone to talk to, she could sit there all day.

I pulled off my top and ran into the sea, the water was freezing, but was a welcome relief after the hot drive down, Dilan and Emir were already in the sea, splashing each other, and shouting loudly.

"Do you remember what Dede used to say Aziz", Dilan said laughing. My grandfather would often give us little pearls of wisdom.

"Yeah, if you do a poo in the sea, make sure you dive under the water once you're done, or else it will follow you, why you are doing one now?" I replied.

"Maybe" Dilan replied as we all began laughing out loud.

"Or refuse, and then slap a man if he tries to shake your hand with his left hand," Emir said still laughing. This was one that my grandfather would repeat over, and over again.

Many Muslims wash after going to the toilet. Traditionally they used their left hand for cleaning, and their right hand for eating, so if someone handed you their left hand, it was a disguised insult.

"Let's swim out to deeper waters," Dilan said as he turned, and began to swim freestyle. After a short distance, we could see Dilan standing, it looked like he was walking on water, whereas he actually was standing on a rock formation.

As I climbed onto the rock, I recalled all the advice we were given over the years, "Don't go out too far, be careful of whirlpools, don't dive under or go into the underwater caverns".

★

After a little while, I went back to the shore. I saw my father away from the group, making sandcastles with Yaffa.

Even though I had promised my mother, this was my father, and I wanted him to know that I was there for him.

Before I walked over to them, I went to where the majority of the family were sitting, under the large parasol. I went to get my wallet, as I had a plan.

"Sila, why don't you go with Yaffa to buy everyone Dondurma?"

"What am I, your slave" Sila replied

"Okay don't then," I said. Realising that she wouldn't get any free ice cream, she reconsidered and agreed to go.

We walked over to Yaffa, and my father "Great castle Dad, not bad for an accountant", I said laughing. Sila took Yaffa off with her, and my father turned to me.

"Aziz your mother told me that you know," he said. My parents knew me too well, and telling me something this big, I was unlikely to let this go.

"Sorry Dad, but I wish you guys had told me."

"Why? You have your life, I don't want my children to worry about me."

"Dad, you are my father, I deserve to know, good or bad, and I am able to make my own decisions."

"Aziz, I know you too well! If I had told you, you would have moved straight back to Los Angeles. You know we want you back home, but not because of this, but because you are ready to come back."

"Dad, of course, I would, I need to be there for my family."

"Son, you are here for us, please don't worry, I will be all right."

I wanted to say so much more. However, Yaffa returned with her ice cream in her hand.

After eating some of Sila's dondurma to her disgust, I convinced her to come into the sea with me. "Come on little Sis, don't worry about your hair, and come into the sea."

We swam out to Dilan and Emir, who had been diving into the underwater caves. As we got closer, Dilan said, "Come on Aziz, let's go under."

"It's too dangerous Dilan, plus we should have brought snorkelling gear."

"You are such a baby Aziz", with that both Dilan and Emir dived under.

"Come on Aziz," Sila said.

Realising that I wasn't going to go, Sila dived under. They were under the water for ten to fifteen minutes when they finally reappeared. I didn't understand why everyone found the caves so interesting.

I had climbed onto a rock, and in the distance, I thought I saw a fin. Though we were not that far off from the beach, I had an irrational fear of sharks.

I had never been attacked or even had an encounter, but I was a child of the Jaws era. Immediately I began to swim back to shore in a mad panic.

I was so panicked that I didn't see a huge wave coming, bringing with it tonnes of seaweed. I was close to the beach, but still panicked, I began running through the thick seaweed.

As I emerged from the beach, relieved I was alive, but once out of the water, I could immediately hear everyone on the beach laughing at me.

The seaweed was all over me, and I looked like the swamp thing. I began pulling it off, huffing and puffing, which only fuelled the laughter.

After my ordeal I refused to go back into the water, preferring to spend my time on the beach. Once we had our picnic, and relaxed some more, it was time to head back to the house. Unfortunately, the Volkswagen decided to break down on the way.

After Dilan, Emir, Sila, Sevda and I pushed it, for what seemed like an eternity, the car restarted. I could just imagine uncle Ilhan laughing, watching us push this old heap of a car.

Once we were back at the house, I offered to take the 7 seater back to Serdar.

I went alone as everyone was too eager to get showered after sitting covered in sand and sea water for so long.

As I pulled up to the garage, Serdar came out to greet me "Aziz, long time no see, how are you?"

"I am good thank you uncle and you?" Serdar was looking a lot older than I had remembered. His garage was large but was full of old car parts scattered all around the front, and rear of the building. It actually looked more like a scrap yard than a garage.

"It is strange, but it feels weird knowing that I won't see uncle anymore," Serdar said.

"I know, I keep expecting him to come out, and shout at me about something," I stated with a smile on my face.

"I know, but he was very proud of all of you, especially you Aziz, he would often come for coffee and tell me what you were up to", I appreciated what Serdar said, thanked him and decided to take a slow walk back to the house.

When I arrived back to the house, there was a queue for the bathroom, but by now people were spending less time in the shower given how cold the water was.

I finally managed to have a shower, and after getting dressed, I went into the kitchen where everyone was already sitting down around the table having a large family meal.

For the whole night, I kept on having to peel myself away from aunt Lale, who kept on hugging me, telling me how much she missed me.

On one occasion, I caught my mother's eye, she looked, and tried to smile, but it was clearly a smile hiding her pain. Listening to uncle Ilhan going on about what he had been up to for over an hour, I decided to head to bed, as I had to be up early to catch my flight.

After kissing everyone goodnight, I got back to the bedroom to find Dilan already sitting there.

"You are a pain, but I miss you cuz, I wish you would come back to LA," he said sincerely.

"I know Dilan, I miss you too."

"I am really sorry about your Dad, I really hope he is going to be okay. I don't know what I would do without him", with that Dilan came over, and hugged me.

★

When the alarm sounded at 6.30am, I was already awake, and quickly pressed the snooze button, so as not to wake my two cousins who were still fast asleep.

After packing the last of my bags, and having a quick cold shower, I walked into the kitchen to find my grandmother, mother, father and Sila all sitting there.

"What are you all doing up?" I said

"We are taking you to the airport Aziz" my mother replied.

"Don't be silly, go back to bed it is too early". Though I protested, no one listened.

In the car going to the airport, my grandmother was sitting next to me, and was holding my arm firmly, like she didn't want to let me go. As we came closer to the airport, she began gently rubbed my arm, I think it was more reassurance for her than me.

After checking in, we all got a coffee.

"Aziz, Nene is going to come to LA to stay with us for a while," my mother said.

"That is really good, I will be over to LA soon Nene", I said. In all of the drama, I had pushed the fact that my grandmother might have been alone had she stayed in Cyprus; I was glad she was going to be with my parents.

I didn't want to leave, so I stayed with my family right up to the last moment, until the final boarding call was made.

As I walked on the tarmac to the plane, I looked back and saw my family standing there waving at me; my mother, grandmother, and sister were all crying.

I waved one last time as I boarded the plane, and as I looked at them, I thought how lucky I was to have them, even uncle Ilhan.

I knew I had a busy time ahead of me, as I had to go to London, and start making preparations to go back to Los Angeles to be with my family.

⭐ ⭐ ⭐

ABOUT THE AUTHOR

⭐ ⭐ ⭐

Atilla Tiriyaki published his debut novel, Cypriana in 2017. The book draws inspiration from Atilla's own life, as he, himself, comes from a diverse background. Growing up in London, and coming from a Turkish Cypriot family, provided him with a great insight to help in the creation and development of the key characters within the story.

Atilla made a career writing technical documentation within large corporations. It was a career break in 2016, which gave him the opportunity to create his first fictional book. A well-travelled individual, visiting over 50 countries, has provided him with opportunities to not only have a wealth of experiences, but to also observe a broad range of characters, and personalities.

"While researching for my book, it surprised me, how little is known or is published with regards to the amazing culture and colourful characters of Northern Cyprus. A lot of people don't realise that Northern Cypriots have their own identity, strong national pride, great sense of humour, and distinct dialect of Turkish" Atilla Tiriyaki

Atilla's love of reading, and travelling, coupled with his observational and storytelling skills provides a style and experience for the reader that is both engaging and easy to follow. The author has a number of writing projects in the pipeline, so watch this space for future releases.